THE TOTALLY AWESOME WORLD OF

STEPH CURRY

LEARN ALL THERE IS TO KNOW ABOUT YOUR FAVORITE MVP

—

NEAL E. FISCHER

becker&mayer! kids

CONTENTS

INTRODUCTION:
2,974

**t was a Tuesday in December 2021.** Nearly 20,000 fans crowded into Madison Square Garden to watch the New York Knicks battle the Golden State Warriors. This wasn't just another game; it was a night that fans and NBA legends knew would be etched in history. It didn't matter what jersey you wore or what team you supported, you were there for one person and one person only: Stephen Curry.

Madison Square Garden

Madison Square Garden, known as "The Garden," "The Mecca of Basketball," or simply MSG, is one of the world's most iconic arenas. Opened on February 11, 1968, in Midtown Manhattan, it's home to the New York Knicks (NBA) and the New York Rangers (NHL) and is the oldest arena in both leagues. This legendary venue has hosted some of history's most famous events, like the "Fight of the Century" between Muhammad Ali and Joe Frazier in 1971, concerts by Elvis Presley, Bruce Springsteen, and Billy Joel, and the first-ever WrestleMania in 1985.

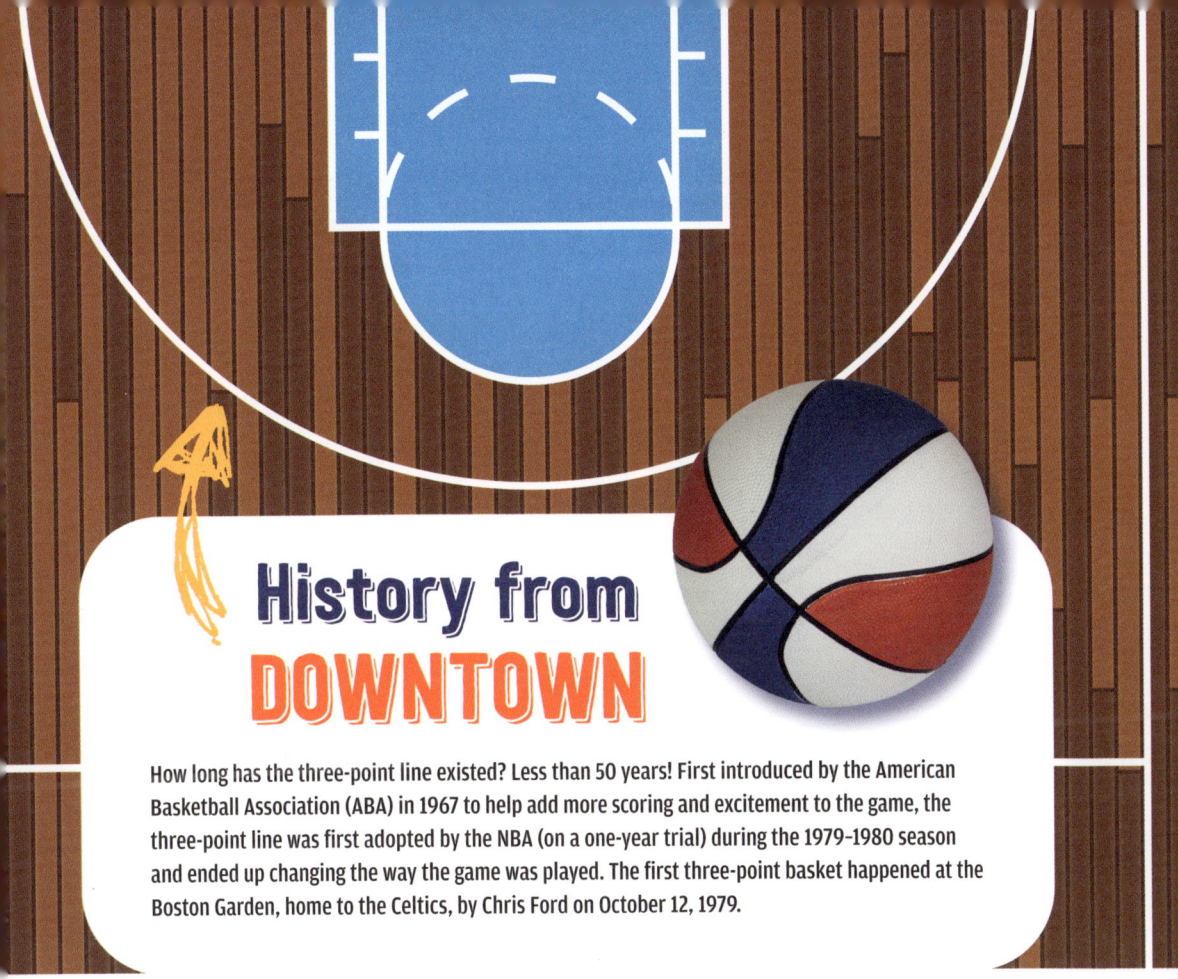

History from
DOWNTOWN

How long has the three-point line existed? Less than 50 years! First introduced by the American Basketball Association (ABA) in 1967 to help add more scoring and excitement to the game, the three-point line was first adopted by the NBA (on a one-year trial) during the 1979-1980 season and ended up changing the way the game was played. The first three-point basket happened at the Boston Garden, home to the Celtics, by Chris Ford on October 12, 1979.

It was the first quarter of the game, and after making his first three-pointer from deep, Stephen ("Steph") Curry was one shot away from breaking Ray Allen's all-time record of 2,973 three-pointers, a record that had stood for ten years. With seven minutes and thirty-three seconds remaining in the first quarter, Alec Burks passed the ball to Andrew Wiggins in the paint, who, in turn, dished the ball out to Steph on the right wing, 28 feet (8.5 m) from the basket. With the fluidity and quick release shot mechanics that have become his signature, Steph released his shot. The crowd held its breath. Then—swish! It was three-pointer number 2,974. Steph Curry was officially the greatest shooter in NBA history.

Coach Steve Kerr called a time-out so Steph could savor the moment. The crowd gave Steph a standing ovation, celebrating not just the record, or a shot, but an era of basketball ushered in by the once scrawny kid out of Davidson College.

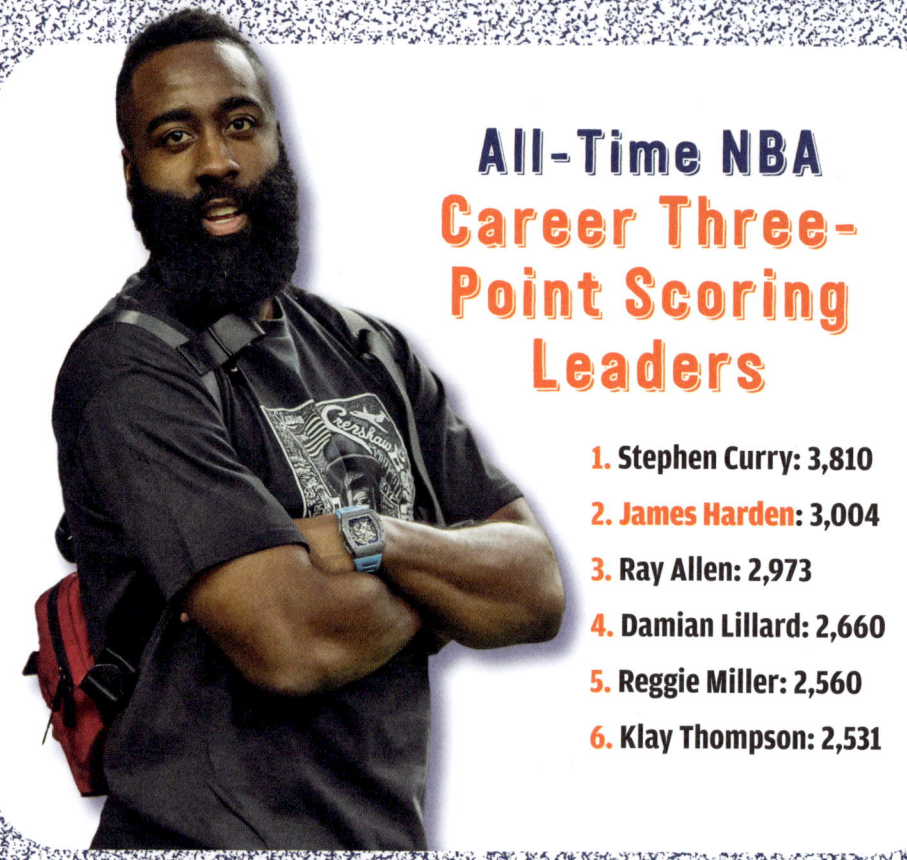

All-Time NBA
Career Three-Point Scoring Leaders

1. **Stephen Curry:** 3,810
2. **James Harden:** 3,004
3. **Ray Allen:** 2,973
4. **Damian Lillard:** 2,660
5. **Reggie Miller:** 2,560
6. **Klay Thompson:** 2,531

In attendance at that momentous game were two people that Steph had looked up to as a kid: Reggie Miller and Ray Allen, some of the game's greatest sharpshooters who'd paved the way for the three-point shot to be taken seriously. As strange as it sounds today, it had in fact initially been dismissed by players and coaches who hadn't grown up with it and believed closer shots were better. But among those that embraced it were Miller and Allen, who were there this magical night to honor the man who took the three-point shot, and the game of basketball, to new heights. Miller summed it up later by saying it was just like Babe Ruth changing baseball with the home run—Steph Curry changed basketball with the three-pointer.

Steph's family was also there for his big night: his mother, Sonya Curry, who remembered all the hours he spent practicing; Dell Curry, Steph's father and a former NBA player, who had helped him master his shot; Bob McKillop, Steph's college coach and mentor; and Steve Kerr, Steph's coach who was also a three-point specialist himself, with the record for highest completion percentage. Steph took a moment to sit down and started to tear up as the crowd looked on. This wasn't just a record; it was a culmination of years of hard work, hours and hours of practice, endless dedication, and love for the game.

So how did Steph become the master of the three-pointer? How did a kid from a small college in North Carolina change the face of basketball? To understand the man behind the record, we have to go back to where it all began . . .

CHAPTER

EARLY LIFE

IT ALL BEGINS

t was 1988. The Los Angeles Dodgers (led by league MVP Kirk Gibson) won the World Series over the Oakland Athletics; the Winter and Summer Olympics both happened that same year; and Margaret Thatcher became the longest-serving British Prime Minister of the twentieth century. Despite famous faces like NFL Quarterbacks Matthew Stafford and Russell Wilson, singers Rihanna and Adele, and mixed-martial artist Conor McGregor all being born this year, the trajectory of the pro sports landscape changing forever was set when the greatest shooter to ever step foot on a basketball court was born in the third month of that year.

Wardell Stephen Curry II was born on March 14, 1988, in Akron, Ohio. He was named after his father, though the world would come to know him as Stephen (pronounced STEFF-en) Curry and friends and family simply called him Steph. Baby Steph came into the world at Akron City Hospital (now Summa Health System) which, in the 1980s, would be responsible for changing the game of basketball forever twice!

Just 39 months before Steph was born, NBA legend LeBron James was born in the same hospital. Years later, one of its many doctors would joke with prospective parents that if they wanted their kid to be an NBA player, they should get delivered in Akron at this hospital.

Greetings from AKRON OHIO

about AKRON, OHIO

- In 1962, **John Glenn** became the first American to orbit the planet. His space suit was made in Akron. The state of Ohio has also produced more astronauts than any other state, including Neil Armstrong, Jim Lovell, John Glenn, and Nancy J. Currie-Gregg.

- Akron was once called the "Rubber Capital of the World" because big tire companies like Goodyear, BFGoodrich, and Firestone all once called the city home. The **Goodyear Blimp** is also stored in Akron!

- The city is home to the All-American Soap Box Derby, where kids race homemade cars down a hill, using nothing but gravity to get their car going up to 35 miles per hour without an engine.

- Sojourner Truth, a famous American abolitionist (meaning someone who wants to end slavery), gave her famous "Ain't I A Woman?" speech in Akron in 1851 at the Ohio Women's Rights Convention.

- The name Akron comes from the Greek word *akron*, which means high point or summit, which makes sense, because the city is at the highest point on the Ohio and Erie Canal.

Steph's father, Dell Curry, was an NBA player who, right before Steph's birth, was playing his first and only season with the Cleveland Cavaliers after being traded from the Utah Jazz. Steph's mother, Sonya, was an accomplished volleyball player and athlete who met Dell while they were both students at Virginia Tech. Although the family thought they'd be calling Akron home, the NBA had a different plan. A brand-new expansion team had joined the league and signed Dell, who was a great sharpshooter (sound familiar?), so the family found themselves headed to Charlotte, North Carolina. Later, Steph would be joined by his brother, Seth (an NBA player), and sister, Sydel (a volleyball player), to round out the athletic Curry family.

What Is an
Expansion Team?

An expansion team is a new team added to a sports league because the league wants to increase the number of teams, or they want to reach new markets or fans that never had a team. The Charlotte Hornets joined the NBA as an expansion team in 1988. Some other famous expansion teams from across sports are the NBA's Toronto Raptors (1995), the NFL's Carolina Panthers (1995), the MLB's Arizona Diamondbacks (1998)—who won the World Series in 2001 just three years after being created—and the NHL's Vegas Golden Knights, who reached the Stanley Cup Finals in their first season.

Charlotte wasn't just a new home for the Currys. It was an opportunity for Dell to make a name for himself with the Charlotte Hornets. It was also the backdrop against which Steph's love for basketball would flourish. When Steph grabbed a basketball in North Carolina at the age of five, that was it.

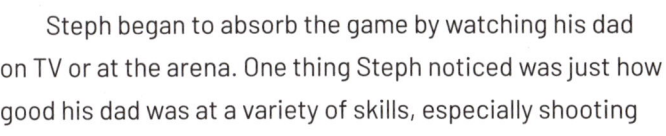

Steph began to absorb the game by watching his dad on TV or at the arena. One thing Steph noticed was just how good his dad was at a variety of skills, especially shooting three-pointers. At one point of his career, Dell Curry was named Sixth Man of the Year. A Sixth Man is a key player who comes off the bench (usually the first one subbed in) and often plays just as many minutes as the other starters. They're

known for their versatility and impact and can change the game's momentum. So it's not hard to figure out where Steph got his versatile playing style from!

But perhaps the most influential person to Steph's development was his mother, Sonya, who played a pivotal role in shaping Steph's character, which would define him on and off the court. As a former athlete, Sonya understood the importance of teamwork and knew what kind of discipline would be required for Steph to be a champion in life and sports.

While Dell was playing in the NBA, Sonya founded a Christian Montessori school in Charlotte so that she could be front and center in Steph's and his siblings' development. There, Sonya instilled the structure of God first, family second, and school third. When Steph once didn't do his chores around the house, Sonya kept him home from a big basketball game as punishment. Her lesson was that you must take ownership of your responsibilities, because if you don't do your part within a family (or a team), it will affect everything else. While Dell may have taught Steph his shot and the fundamentals needed to be a fierce competitor, Sonya was the one who gave the athlete his work ethic and the discipline that he carries with him today.

IF YOU COULD

invent a chore that everyone would actually enjoy doing, what would it be? If you could trade any chore for another, would you do it?

Steph wanted to be a basketball player more than anything, but he was often the smallest player on the court. His clothes always seemed too big, the ball seemed gigantic in his hands, and he was practically in the shadow of the players who

guarded him. But Steph realized early on that if he couldn't control how tall he was, he'd have to focus on what he could control: ball-handling, shooting, speed, and agility. Luckily for him, he had a great role model at Dell's office named **Muggsy Bogues**. Muggsy was the shortest player in NBA history, as the 5-feet, 3-inch point guard for the Charlotte Hornets, and he showed that heart and skill can triumph over physical

limitations. He quickly became one of Steph's favorite players, and his influence before, during, and after games was profound. Steph learned that it didn't matter how tall he was if he could shoot from anywhere on the court and be an assassin with the ball.

A Taste of Fame

In the 1990s, Dell was a fan favorite and a recognizable face on and off the court—especially after starring in a series of commercials for Burger King. But his young, bright-eyed costar makes the commercials memorable all these years later. Little Steph Curry appeared in the commercials with his dad, delivering memorable lines like, "Bring home the bacon, Dad!" This opportunity wasn't just a fun family activity, but a learning experience for Steph. He saw how his dad handled the spotlight and remained a professional.

Steph began playing basketball nonstop. After homework? Shooting baskets. After chores? Shooting baskets. Rain or shine, he was shooting baskets. As Steph honed his skills and made up for his small stature, he also played in tournaments against opponents who were much bigger and stronger than him. But all anyone could talk about was how good that Curry kid was. When Steph was about 10 years old, a young player who practically towered over Steph watched in awe as Steph shot. That player was Kevin Durant. But the tournaments would have to be put on hold, because in 1999, Dell was traded to the Toronto Raptors, which meant the Curry family had to pack up and move north.

DID YOU KNOW?

Canada Edition

Learn a bit more aboot the Great White North, eh!

- The maple leaf is Canada's national symbol (it's on their flag), the beaver is their national animal, and—no surprise—hockey is their national sport.

- Canada has more lakes than any other country in the world.

- Churchill, Manitoba, is known as the Polar Bear Capital of the World.

- Famous people from Canada include Keanu Reeves, Ryan Gosling, Drake, Justin Bieber, Jim Carrey, The Weeknd, Michael Bublé, Martin Short, and Ryan Reynolds.

- Do you like pancakes and waffles? Seventy-one percent of the world's maple syrup comes from Canada.

GRR...

LIFE IN
CANADA

Living in Toronto introduced Steph to a whole new world of basketball. The Raptors were another expansion team and had just started playing in the city a few years earlier, so Toronto was alive with excitement for the NBA. Dell would often bring his sons to Raptors games, and Steph would shoot around during pregame or halftime, soaking in the atmosphere of the arena and always taking mental notes.

At the time, **Vince Carter** (now a Hall of Famer) was one of the Raptors' biggest stars, known for his explosive dunks and high-flying gameplay. He recognized something special in Steph and took him under his wing. Before games or after practices, Steph would play Vince one-on-one. Vince liked to joke that he would finish a tough workout or practice, and around the corner, every time, was little Steph asking him, "Are you ready? Are you ready?" Eventually, Steph became so good that Carter had to start seriously defending against him, watching in amazement as Steph sank deep three after deep three. These sessions weren't just about playing basketball; they were about learning what it took to succeed at the highest levels and trusting your teachers—lessons that would stick with Steph throughout his career.

Steph's development took a huge turn away from the Raptors' practice court when he enrolled at Queensway Christian College, playing under Coach James Lackey. Coach Lackey was initially not super enthusiastic about his new 5-feet, 4-inch eighth grader. But from the moment 13-year-old Steph stepped on the court in Canada, it was clear to everyone—Lackey, the players, the parents, the league—that he was a special talent. Steph was a scoring machine, effortlessly sinking shots from every spot imaginable. All those days shooting in the pouring rain and sharpening his skills with NBA legends had paid off. Steph would lead Queensway's basketball team as their leader and top scorer into an undefeated 2001–2002 season, his first and last with the Saints.

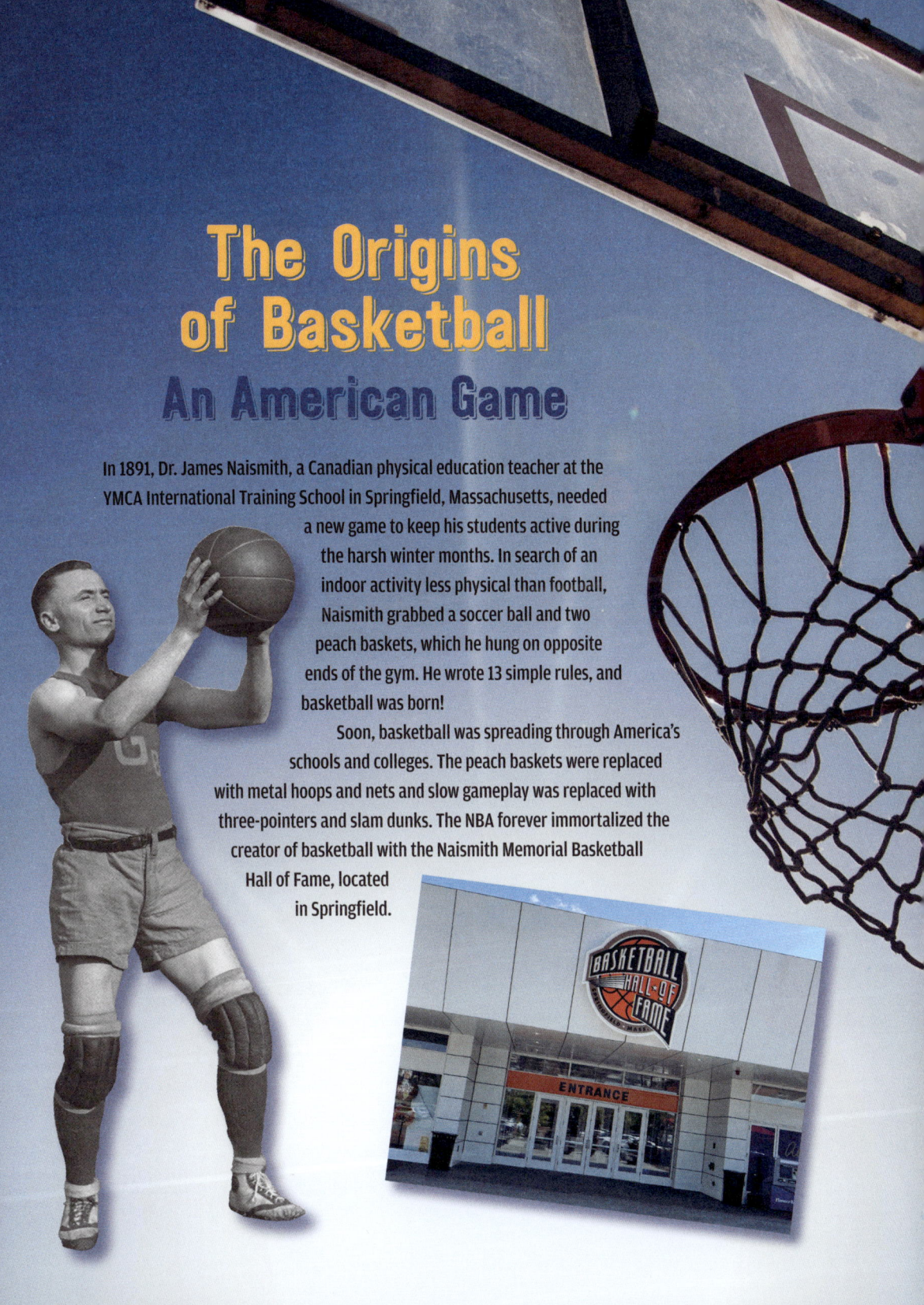

The Origins of Basketball

An American Game

In 1891, Dr. James Naismith, a Canadian physical education teacher at the YMCA International Training School in Springfield, Massachusetts, needed a new game to keep his students active during the harsh winter months. In search of an indoor activity less physical than football, Naismith grabbed a soccer ball and two peach baskets, which he hung on opposite ends of the gym. He wrote 13 simple rules, and basketball was born!

Soon, basketball was spreading through America's schools and colleges. The peach baskets were replaced with metal hoops and nets and slow gameplay was replaced with three-pointers and slam dunks. The NBA forever immortalized the creator of basketball with the Naismith Memorial Basketball Hall of Fame, located in Springfield.

One game from that season stuck out to Lackey. The team was down six or seven points with just about a minute left on the clock. Lackey called timeout to give his team a pep talk about being a good sport, win or lose—but Steph wasn't having it. He interrupted his coach mid-speech and declared, "We are not going to lose this game. Give me the ball and we will win." Over the final minute of the game, Steph scored nine points, erasing the deficit and securing a win for Queensway by six points.

After three years playing for the Toronto Raptors and 16 seasons total in the NBA, Steph's dad, Dell, decided that it was time to retire. Dell retired as the Charlotte Hornets' all-time leader in games (701) and two-point field goals (3,022), as well as finishing second in total points scored (9,839) and second in three-point field goals (929). Dell and Sonya decided that they wanted to move their family back to Charlotte, where Dell had spent most of his career and Sonya had started a successful school. What did that mean for Steph? He'd be facing much tougher competition in America both on and off the court, including . . . high school.

The Basics of Basketball

Don't know the positions of a basketball starting five? Here's a quick cheat sheet:

POINT GUARD (PG): Think of the point guard as the team's quarterback or floor general. They handle the ball the most and make sure everyone's in position.
Famous point guards: Steph Curry, Magic Johnson, Steve Nash

SHOOTING GUARD (SG): Usually the team's best shooter or scorer. They look for ways to make buckets from anywhere and help the point guard with ball handling and passing.
Famous shooting guards: Michael Jordan, Kobe Bryant, Anthony Edwards

SMALL FORWARD (SF): A versatile player who is good at just about everything. They are very athletic and play both close to the basket and on the outside.
Famous small forwards: LeBron James, Larry Bird, Scottie Pippen

POWER FORWARD (PF): One of the bigger, stronger players, and more physical than the small forward. PFs often play close to the basket and are great at grabbing rebounds and scoring from inside the paint.
Famous power forwards: Giannis Antetokounmpo, Tim Duncan, Karl Malone

Center (C): Typically, the tallest player on the team, playing right near the basket. They block shots, grab rebounds, and score from close range.
Famous centers: Nikola Jokic, Shaquille O'Neal, Kareem Abdul-Jabbar

CHAPTER

SWOOSH

BACK HOME TO
CHARLOTTE

Steph was about to begin a new chapter in his life in North Carolina. He enrolled at Charlotte Christian School, a high school with a little over 1,000 students. Gone were the days of being the star player in Canada and leading his team to victory by scoring 50 points a game. He was back in America, where the competition would be fiercer and the players bigger, stronger, and more skilled. As he settled in at his new school, he realized that it was a different, very competitive world, where talent alone wouldn't be enough. He had the skills, but not the confidence.

DID YOU KNOW

Michael Jordan, the greatest basketball player ever and a North Carolina native, didn't get the opportunity to shine early in high school either? He was placed on the JV team as a sophomore due to being too short (like Steph) and because coaches felt he wasn't ready to play varsity. This gave Michael a chip on his shoulder and made him work harder to get better.

Because of that, Steph didn't even try out for the varsity team in his freshmen year. He was nervous and went out for junior varsity (JV) instead, so he didn't have to put himself out there. The coaches were watching, though, and saw potential in Steph including his unique blend of skill and intelligence. What he lacked in size, he more than made up for with his work ethic and passion for the game.

But there was one aspect of Steph's size that he couldn't overcome with drive, ambition, and heart: getting the jersey he wanted. Steph wanted to wear number 30, just like his dad, but there was a problem: the higher the number, the bigger the jersey from the manufacturer. Instead of swimming in the number 30 jersey, Steph settled for number 20, a number that would later become one to remember.

Most Famous
#20s
in Sports History

NFL

Barry Sanders (Detroit Lions), Hall of Fame running back
Ed Reed (Baltimore Ravens), Hall of Fame safety

NBA

Gary Payton (Seattle SuperSonics), Hall of Fame point guard
Manu Ginobili (San Antonio Spurs), Four-time NBA champion

MLB

Frank Robinson (Cincinnati Reds,
Baltimore Orioles),
Hall of Fame outfielder
Mike Schmidt (Philadelphia Phillies),
Hall of Fame third baseman

NHL

Luc Robitaille (Los Angeles Kings),
Hall of Fame left winger
Bob Gainey (Montreal Canadiens),
Hall of Fame forward

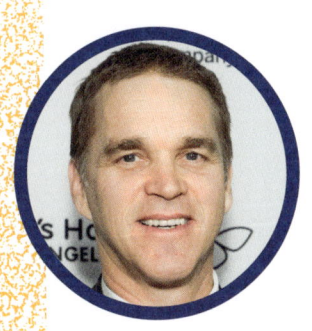

THE SUMMER OF
TEARS

uring Steph's sophomore year of high school, his father, Dell, noticed that Steph's shot would need to be completely overhauled if he had any chance at playing in college or the pros. Steph had developed a habit of shooting from his waist, almost from the belt buckle, in order to generate enough power to get the ball in the air. Despite making most of his shots, his shooting form would make it too easy for taller and stronger opponents to guard and block him. That summer, which they dubbed "The Summer of Tears," focused on rebuilding both Steph's shot and his confidence so he could become a more efficient shooter.

! TOTALLY AWESOME !
STATS

- Steph holds the record for most three-pointers in a single NBA season: 402.
- With a career three-point shooting percentage of about 0.426 (or 42.6%), Steph is one of the most accurate long-range shooters ever. The all-time number 1 on that list is Steph's coach, Steve Kerr.
- Steph is celebrated for his ability to shoot "logo threes," or shots from extremely long distances. During the 2018–2019 season, he made 54% of shots from 30–35 feet (9.1–10.7 m), which makes him basically impossible to guard.
- Steph has made over 20 game-winning or game-tying shots in the final 24 seconds of regular-season games. If time is running out, give Steph the ball!
- In playoff games, Steph has hit at least one three-pointer in 133 consecutive games, the longest streak in NBA history.

Over that difficult high school summer, Steph spent hours deconstructing the low, inefficient shot and building one that had a higher release above his head. The physical part was hard for Steph, but even harder was the mental battle. Steph has said it was the worst summer of his life. He felt frustrated, defeated, and angry, even asking his parents why he had to do it at all. His mother, Sonya, played a crucial role in keeping him motivated, offering encouragement and reminding him of the bigger picture. She told Steph that if it was too frustrating to learn this new technique, he could just keep his old shot. But if he bought into what his dad was teaching him, he needed to stick with it, and with hard work and perseverance, it would all pay off.

MICHIGAN STATE

once played North Carolina aboard the USS *Carl Vinson* (a Navy aircraft carrier) in one of history's most unique basketball games, what became known as the Carrier Classic. The players were surrounded by fighter jets and over seven thousand spectators, including President Barack Obama!

Off the court, Steph's time in high school was transformative in ways he couldn't have imagined at the time. When he was 15 years old, he met a 14-year-old girl named Ayesha Alexander, whose family had just moved to Charlotte from Canada. They bonded over their shared love of Maynards, a Canadian candy. While all the girls had a crush on Steph because he was kind, funny, silly, and charismatic, Ayesha firmly wrote at the bottom of her notebook, "No athletes because they're arrogant." Little did she know that

these interactions at their church youth group would just be the start of their story together.

When Steph returned for junior year after his Summer of Tears, he was a completely different player. He was taller (thanks, growth spurt!), stronger, and his shot looked a lot different. But most of all, he had renewed confidence. Those grueling hours spent practicing with Dell had paid off. His new shot was a thing of beauty: quick, efficient, but most of all, deadly accurate. At 6 feet, 2 inches, he was still one of the smaller players on the team, but he was no longer the scrawny kid who had to settle for jersey number 20 because he was too small.

Steph's newfound confidence quickly made him one of the leaders on the team. He was the first one in the gym and the last one to leave, often taking hundreds of shots in practice to be as accurate as he could be for his team. During the school day, he was engaged and always interested in learning, focusing on his schoolwork, his faith, and his sports equally.

Getting Dramatic

Building strong relationships with your teachers and exploring many different subjects and interests is very important, as Steph shows us. During high school, Steph had a strong interest in theater and enjoyed developing new skills like costume design, set construction, and creating posters for school plays. One of his most meaningful connections was with his drama, film, and broadcasting teacher, Chad Fair, who quickly recognized Steph's dedication to his schoolwork and the arts. Their friendship has endured for many years, and when Steph was chosen by nonprofit organization, TeachersCount—which promotes awareness of the vital role educators play in shaping individuals and society—for their public service campaign "Behind Every Famous Person is a Fabulous Teacher," he chose Fair to be honored.

Steph had a reputation for being one of the best shooters in the state, but major colleges recruiting for their programs were hesitant to take a chance on him. It was the same old story: he was too small, too scrawny, not durable. What hurt most was that Virginia Tech, the school where his mother and father played their respective sports, showed little interest, offering him only a walk-on spot. Steph watched players who were bigger but less skilled receive full-ride scholarships (meaning all fees are paid) from all the big programs. But the most important thing Steph did was not let any of this discourage him. Instead, he used it as motivation.

FROM UNDERRATED TO
UNBELIEVABLE

With offers from big schools failing to materialize, Steph's hopes of playing Division I basketball (aka the top level of college basketball) began to fade. But then a sliver of hope appeared. **Bob McKillop**, the head coach at Davidson College in North Carolina, a small Division I college, was following Steph's high school career closely and recognized something that everyone else overlooked. He also already knew of Steph thanks to another sport: baseball. Steph had played with McKillop's son Brendan on an AAU team (Amateur Athletic Union) of 10-year-olds that had won the North Carolina state championship many years earlier. But it all clicked for McKillop when he watched Steph in a tournament when his team was losing. He saw how

Steph's Yearbook Quotes

In Steph's senior yearbook, there are two quotes next to his picture. The first is a quote by Michael Jordan:

"I've always believed that if you put in the work, the results will come. I don't do things half-heartedly. Because I know if I do, then I can expect half-hearted results."

The second reads:

Will be remembered as...

...swoosh

...baller

...sweet to everyone

Steph handled himself and encouraged his teammates instead of giving up. He looked beyond Steph's size and focused, instead, on his shooting ability, unbeatable work ethic, and basketball IQ. He thought Steph could be a game changer for Davidson and wanted to build his entire program around Steph.

THE START OF
SOMETHING SPECIAL

Steph's decision to commit to Davidson was the true beginning of his rise to legendary status. Like Steph, Davidson was also an underdog in the world of collegiate sports. For both Steph and Davidson, the next four years wouldn't just be about playing basketball. They would be about proving they had what it takes to be champions.

DAVIDSON COLLEGE, located in Davidson, North Carolina, is a small liberal arts college known for its attention to academics and its close-knit community. Currently, about 1,900 students attend Davidson. To put that into context, Davidson's Division I teams might face big schools like Texas A&M, Ohio State University, or University of Central Florida, which each have over 60,000 students!

Davidson wasn't a powerhouse school. It was a more intimate campus known more for its academics than its sports. But that was what Steph needed, a place where he could shine as a student, touch the hearts and minds of his classmates with his kindness, wittiness, and care, and show his stuff on the court while proving all his doubters wrong. Meanwhile, Sonya Curry's biggest request to Coach McKillop before Steph joined Davidson was to keep him accountable. And on the first day of practice, McKillop did just that: when Steph was 90 seconds

late, McKillop sent him to the showers immediately and made him play catchup the next day. Steph learned his lesson—he was never late again.

In Steph's first collegiate game against Eastern Michigan, he finished with 15 points but committed a staggering 13 turnovers. It wasn't quite the start Coach McKillop (or Steph) had imagined. But McKillop did something that Steph never forgot: he didn't bench him. He had confidence in Steph and started him again for the next game against powerhouse Michigan. Steph took that gesture and turned it into 32 points, 9 rebounds, and 4 assists, and his teammates and the conference took notice. Steph found a mentor in Coach McKillop from that day on, and their close relationship would change the direction of Steph's life.

A National Obsession

March Madness is the nickname for the NCAA Men's Basketball Tournament, one of the most exciting and unpredictable sports events in the country. Every March, 68 college teams from across the country compete in a single-elimination tournament to determine the national champion. The "madness" refers to both the fandom surrounding the event and the famous upsets that happen every year. With millions of fans filling out their brackets, trying to predict the winner and watching their favorite teams, March Madness brings the nation (and now the world) together every year.

During his freshman year, Steph led the Southern Conference in scoring
(21.5 points per game) and broke the NCAA freshman record for most three-pointers
made in a single season (he sank 122). The Davidson Wildcats ended with a 29–5
record and even made it to the NCAA tournament, but they unfortunately lost to
Maryland in their first-round match, despite Steph putting up 30 points. That year,
Steph was named Southern Conference Freshman of the Year and the SoCon
Tournament MVP. These early games and accomplishments set the stage for what
was to come.

A CINDERELLA STORY

The 2007–2008 Davidson season was when Steph Curry went from small-town hero to national name. He had reached his full height but still had the baby face that became his trademark. While his scoring average catapulted to 25.9 points per game, what really stood out to everyone was his leadership, his poise in big pressure moments, and his ability to lift his teammates to new heights. During that season's NCAA tournament, Davidson was given the 10th seed and faced off against Gonzaga, the 7th-seeded team, in their first game. Steph scored 40 points in the game, leading Davidson to an 82–76 victory, Davidson's first tournament win since 1969.

In the next round, Davidson faced Georgetown University, a team known for being a storied basketball school, alma mater to NBA legends and loaded with future talent. Early in the game, Georgetown got out to a 17-point lead. But in the second half, Steph scored 25 points and led Davidson to a stunning 74–70 comeback victory. Fans were beginning to fall in love with this unassuming guard from a small school in North Carolina.

NCAA
Underdogs

The NCAA tournament is most famous for teams that defy the odds. Here are some of those stories:

- **North Carolina State (1983):** The Wolfpack was 6th seed and defeated incredible teams like Virginia and Houston to win the championship on a buzzer-beater.

- **Villanova (1985):** The 8th-seeded Wildcats became the lowest-seeded team to win the NCAA title after defeating Georgetown in a thrilling final.

- **George Mason (2006):** The Patriots were an 11th seed and reached the Final Four after a dramatic win in overtime over top-seeded Connecticut.

- **Florida Gulf Coast (2013):** The Eagles were known as "Dunk City," and as a 15th-seeded team, became the first to reach the Sweet 16, dazzling with their flashy play.

- **Loyola Chicago (2018):** The 11th-seeded Ramblers, led by their 98-year-old superfan (and team chaplain) Sister Jean, reached the Final Four, defeating a ton of higher seeded teams along the way.

During this legendary Davidson run, Steph caught the attention of an NBA superstar who would later be integral to his story: LeBron James. When Davidson beat Georgetown and made the Sweet 16 (meaning 16 teams left), LeBron made his way to Ford Field (home of the Detroit Lions) to watch Steph take on third-seeded Wisconsin. Curry put on another spectacle, scoring 33 points in a 73–56 Davidson upset victory. LeBron was captivated by the young star's performance and later, in an interview that would go viral 15 years later, spoke of a bright future for him in the NBA.

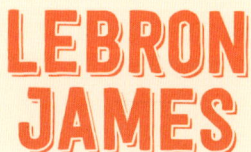

LEBRON JAMES and Steph Curry have appeared in the NBA Finals against each other four times—in a row. Steph has a 15-7 record against LeBron and has won three out of the four championships they've played against each other. (But Steph still has a signed and framed LeBron jersey in his childhood bedroom in North Carolina.)

Davidson made it to the Elite Eight to face the top-seeded Kansas Jayhawks in the toughest game of Steph's life and one of the most thrilling in March Madness history. Steph scored 25 points and hit a crucial three in the final minute, bringing Davidson within two points of victory. Then, Kansas double-teamed Steph and forced him to pass the ball. His teammate took a shot before the buzzer and narrowly missed. The Wildcats magical run ended in a 59–57 loss. That Kansas team went on to win the national championship.

Steph may not have become a champion just yet, but he did become a national sensation and put Davidson's program on the map. LeBron congratulated the Wildcats on a hard-fought battle and great season. Little did either of them know, this was the beginning of this generation's biggest rivalry. Just like Magic Johnson had Larry Bird and Batman has the Joker, Steph Curry and LeBron James would go on to push each other to new heights and make the NBA what it is today.

That summer, after he appeared on *Late Night with Conan O'Brion* to talk about his newfound stardom, Steph reconnected with his church-youth-group friend **Ayesha Alexander** in Los Angeles. They strolled along Hollywood Boulevard, visited the famous Madame Tussauds wax museum, and drank chai tea lattes. They had an instant connection that would eventually become a partnership in life, love, and business that is still going strong to this day.

Despite fans calling for him to join the NBA, Steph returned to Davidson for his junior year so that he could learn the position of point guard. That year, he led the entire nation in scoring with 28.6 points per game and set an NCAA record for the most three-pointers in a season with 162. But Davidson failed to make the NCAA tournament. It was a bittersweet end to a captivating college career. Steph decided not to go back to Davidson for his senior year to get his degree and instead entered the NBA Draft, where he would be surrounded by the best players in the world.

STEPH HAD PROMISED

his mother to finish his degree, and he didn't forget that promise. In 2022, he returned to Davidson to complete his schooling, writing a thesis on gender equality in sports, which led to his graduation and his jersey being retired by the school.

Basketball
GLOSSARY

Assist: Players get assists when they pass the ball to a teammate who scores. Having lots of assists means you're a great team player!

Block: The ball is blocked when a defender stops a shot by swatting the ball away or blocking the shot before it reaches the basket. If you want to see some great blocking highlights, look up the best to ever do it, Hakeem Olajuwon, who is No. 1 in NBA history with 3,830.

Double-Double: When a player reaches double digits in two categories in a single game. Think 10 points and 10 rebounds, or 10 points and 10 assists.

Dribbling: Bouncing the ball with one hand while moving up and down the court. It's how players move without passing or shooting.

Fast Break: When a team moves the ball down the court very quickly, trying to score before the defense has time to get ready.

Foul: Illegal contact with an opponent results in a foul.

Free Throw: This is an unguarded shot, usually given to a player after they are fouled, that is taken from the free throw line, which is 15 feet (4.6 m) from the backboard. Each free throw attempt is worth 1 point and players get 10 seconds to complete each attempt. Steph Curry is the most accurate free throw shooter of all time!

Rebound: If an attempted shot is missed and a player grabs the ball (if it bounces off the backboard, the rim, or doesn't go in), that is a rebound.

Shot Clock: This is the official timer each team's offense gets to take a shot. After 24 seconds, if they don't shoot, a buzzer sounds and it's a turnover.

Steal: Anytime a player legally takes the ball away from an opponent, they steal the ball. This is a great type of defense and sometimes leads to exciting fast breaks and dunks.

Three-Pointer: A shot that is made from beyond the three-point line, the big semicircle on each side of the court. It measures 22 feet (6.7 m) from the corners and 23 feet, 9 inches (7.2 m) everywhere else.

Turnover: When a team loses possession of the ball to the other team because of things like a steal, a bad pass to a teammate, or the ball going out of bounds.

CHAPTER

BECOMING A WARRIOR

PRE-DRAFT ANALYSIS

Stephen Curry (Davidson College)

SCOUT
Stevan Petrovic, December 15, 2008

NBA COMPARISON
Mahmoud Abdul-Rauf

Far below NBA standard in regard to explosiveness and athleticism. At 6-2, he's extremely small for the NBA shooting guard position, and it will likely keep him from being much of a defender at the next level. Doesn't like when defenses are too physical with him. Not a great finisher around the basket due to his size and physical attributes. Makes some silly mistakes at the PG position. Needs to add some muscles to his upper body but appears as though he'll always be skinny.

Stephen Curry
(Davidson College)

Pre-Draft Scouting Report

"PERCEIVED WEAKNESSES"

Source: Former NBA Head Coach

- Not a true point guard
- Out of control at times
- Shot selection
- Stuck between 1 and 2 (i.e., can't decide if he's a point guard or shooting guard)
- Ability to defend position at next level?
- Lateral quickness
- Versatility to defend multiple positions
- Limited upside?
- Backup/Fringe Starter?
- College system makes him difficult to evaluate
- Average athleticism
- Average size
- Average wingspan
- Frail frame
- Relies too heavily on outside shot

THE DRAFT

The annual NBA Draft is a special night, when hoopers from around the world could have their lives changed in an instant. But on the night of the 2009 draft, the road to that moment had been anything but smooth for Steph. Despite his successes at Davidson, scouts and analysts at the NBA weren't convinced that Steph had the X factor a player needed for the NBA. Steph knew what the scouting reports said about his size and strength, but he didn't let it get to him. Instead, it only fueled his determination.

ONLY FOUR TEAMS in NBA history have never had a No. 1 pick in the draft: the Denver Nuggets, Indiana Pacers, Memphis Grizzlies, and Utah Jazz. The Cleveland Cavaliers have the most No. 1 picks in history.

On June 25, 2009, the night of the NBA Draft—which also happened to be Dell Curry's 45th birthday—Steph waited nervously with his family to see how things would shake out. Steph and his father had their sights set on only one team that night: the New York Knicks. The team had the eighth overall pick and represented the chance for Steph to play at the iconic Madison Square Garden every night, a dream come true.

The first overall pick in the draft was **Blake Griffin** to the Los Angeles Clippers. Pick three was James Harden to the Oklahoma City Thunder. Then, the first and second point guards of the night were taken at five and six by the Minnesota Timberwolves: Ricky Rubio and Jonny Flynn. With these picks, the NBA made it clear who they thought were the best point guards in the league.

There was one more pick to go before Steph's dreams came true. But something else happened first: the Golden State Warriors, picking at seven (despite Steph turning down a workout with them), saw something in him and chose him anyway. Steph Curry was now an NBA point guard, *and* a Top 10 draft pick. But none of that mattered to Steph. His dream job was about to get started.

IF YOU COULD be drafted by any NBA team, who would you want to draft you and why?

GREAT
EXPECTATIONS

Expectations for Steph were sky-high in the NBA. His slender frame seemed out of place in the league, and the veteran players let him know it by treating him a bit rougher. To make matters worse, Steph's rookie season marked the beginning of ankle issues that he would deal with for his entire career. In fact, Steph missed the first game of his rookie season because of a sprained left ankle.

The Warriors as a whole struggled during Steph's rookie year, too, finishing with a losing record, but Steph was the bright spot in a clear rebuild. He earned a starting spot and eventually finished second in Rookie of the Year voting. He was named Western Conference Rookie of the Month for January, March, and April, and was the only rookie to win that honor three times. He scored more than 30 points eight times, the most by a rookie since LeBron James and Carmelo Anthony. Steph ended his season with a then-career high 42 points, 9 rebounds, and 8 assists, the first rookie since 1961 to have those numbers (Oscar Robertson had great stats back then). And if all that wasn't enough, he showed who he was from beyond the arc by netting

STEPH CURRY

is only one of three rookies in professional basketball history to have recorded 29 points, 5 rebounds, and 10 assists on 70% TS (True Shooting Percentage) multiple times. TS is a metric used to measure a player's efficiency at shooting the ball; the higher the percentage, the better the shooter. The only other rookies to accomplish this same feat are Michael Jordan and Caitlin Clark.

166 three-pointers, the most ever by a rookie in history. That record stood for a decade before being broken.

Steph's second season was mostly about his growing confidence. He started to take more risks by dribbling through defenders and making the impossible deep shots he's now known for. He also improved his stats slightly by averaging 18.6 points and 5.8 assists per game and led the NBA in free-throw percentage with an incredible 93.4%—a Warriors record that still stands.

Fans also started to notice another quirk on the court: Steph's mouthguard. He started wearing the protective gear after being elbowed in the face in college. When shooting or doing free-throws, you'll often see Steph chewing on his mouthguard. As Steph told Jimmy Kimmel in an interview, chewing on his mouthguard is a way for him to stay calm and focused in high-pressure moments. Thanks to his chewing, Steph goes through about 12 mouthguards a season!

Sports Superstitions

Many athletes have superstitions or routines that make them feel more comfortable with performing, like these:

- **Michael Jordan** famously wore his University of North Carolina shorts under his Chicago Bulls uniform every game as a good luck charm.

- Hall of Fame baseball player **Wade Boggs** ate chicken before every game, as he thought it made him perform better. The habit started after he won a batting title in 1983 and realized he ate a lot of chicken that year. He kept up the habit, and even earned the nickname "Chicken Man."

- Tennis legend **Serena Williams** wore the same pair of socks through an entire tournament for good luck. She wouldn't change her socks unless she lost. That included Grand Slam tournaments—which can last two weeks!

- Hall of Fame NHL goalie **Patrick Roy** used to talk to his goalposts during games and treated them like friends who would help him keep pucks out of the net. He found it comforting.

- Former NFL kicker **Matt Bryant** had the sweetest of all superstitions—literally! Before every game of his 17-year career, Matt would have a chocolate milkshake for good luck.

HELLO...

But just as Steph was starting to really shine, disaster struck. His troublesome ankles, which had been a concern starting his rookie season, gave out again, causing him to miss a lot of time on the court. During his third season, he was only able to play 26 games. We know Steph Curry now as clutch, electric, dependable, and accurate, but at this point in his career, he became known as "injury-prone," an assessment that can be hard to overcome. Steph's situation became so uncertain that the Warriors nearly traded him to the Milwaukee Bucks in exchange for a player named Andrew Bogut. The Bucks doctor stopped the deal, saying that trading for Curry and his ankles would be too risky.

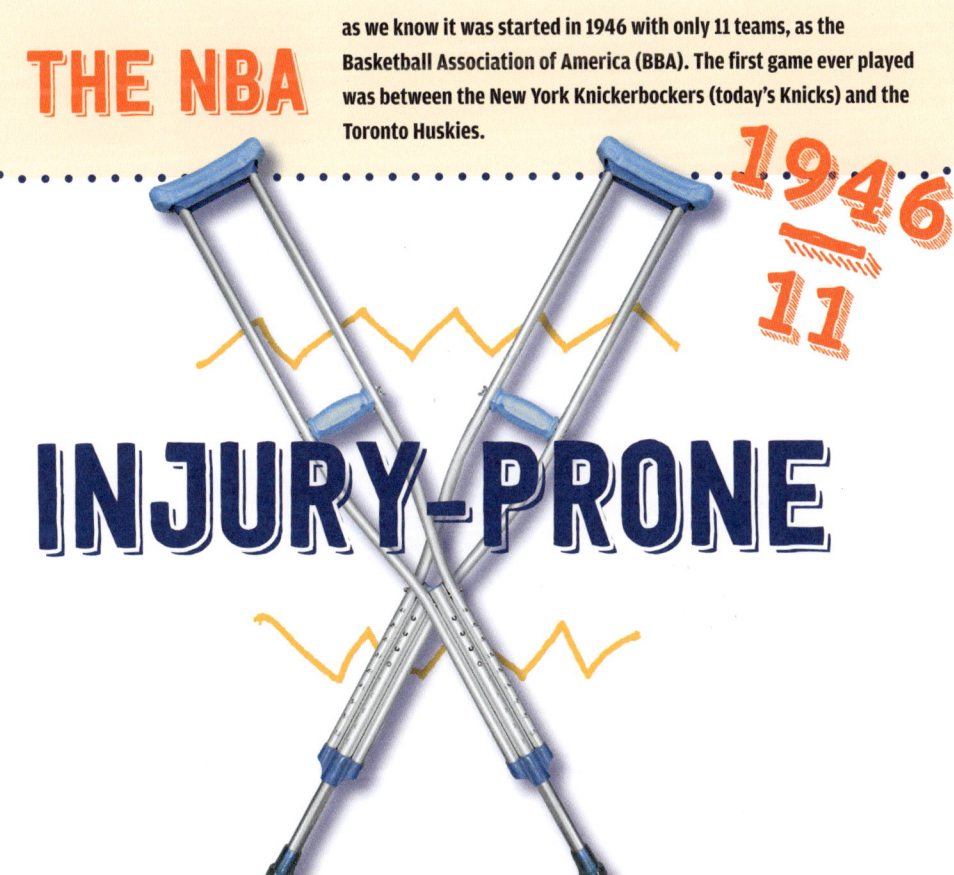

THE NBA as we know it was started in 1946 with only 11 teams, as the Basketball Association of America (BBA). The first game ever played was between the New York Knickerbockers (today's Knicks) and the Toronto Huskies.

1946 / 11

INJURY-PRONE

Golden State fans and the media assumed that this would be the end of Steph's ride with the Warriors, but the team did something no one expected—they instead traded their leader, Monta Ellis. In 2012, the Warriors offered Steph a four-year contract extension worth $44 million. Although fans were outraged by the Ellis trade and many considered the team's agreement with Steph risky, the Warriors saw something special in Steph and still thought that the future of the franchise was building around Steph.

And build they did. That offseason, they drafted Harrison Barnes and Draymond Green, and with second-year guard Klay Thompson starting to flourish, the core of the Golden State Warriors was starting to gel under new coach Mark Jackson. Plus, sponsorships started to roll in for Steph, who put **Under Armour** on the map with his mega deal. Would new players, a new coach, a new identity, a new brand, and a new system of offense first be the winning changes the Warriors needed?

23 pt
7 ast

272 threes

Under Coach Mark Jackson, a former NBA player who had once played with Steph's father, Steph began to flourish. He was the team's lead shooter, averaging 23 points and 7 assists per game, including a 54-point explosion at Madison Square Garden. During the 2012–2013 season, Steph set a new NBA single-season three-point record, hitting 272 threes and breaking Ray Allen's previous mark. That season, the Warriors even got to the playoffs for the first time since 2007 but were defeated in the second round by a very solid and experienced San Antonio Spurs team.

Do Players Make the Best
HEAD COACHES?

Many of the most successful NBA coaches were players first. Just check out this list for proof:

- **Phil Jackson:** Played 11 seasons (1967–1978) primarily with the New York Knicks. Won 11 NBA championships as a coach with the Chicago Bulls and Los Angeles Lakers.

- **Steve Kerr:** Played 15 seasons (1988–2003) and won 5 NBA championships with the Chicago Bulls and San Antonio Spurs. Has won 4 NBA championships as the head coach of the Golden State Warriors—so far!

- **Lenny Wilkens:** Played 15 seasons (1960–1975) and was a 9-time All-Star who coached and played on the same team for 6 years. After retiring as a player in 1975, he won his first championship as a coach in 1979 with the Seattle Supersonics and has 1,332 career wins, which is third all-time behind Don Nelson and Gregg Popovich.

- **Doc Rivers:** Played 13 seasons (1983–1996) as a point guard, mostly with the Atlanta Hawks. Won an NBA championship with the Boston Celtics in 2008 as a coach and has over 1,000 wins.

- **Pat Riley:** Played 9 seasons (1967–1976), primarily with the Los Angeles Lakers. He has won 5 NBA championships as a coach with the Lakers and Miami Heat and is one of the league's most respected figures.

With Steph no longer in Ellis's shadow, and his body getting stronger every year, he became what the team needed most: a playmaker, a leader, and the heart of the Warriors' offense. Teammate **Klay Thompson** was also beginning to flourish, knocking down three-pointers with the same efficiency and flair as Steph. When they clicked, they formed one of the most dangerous backcourts in NBA history and even earned a nickname: the Splash Brothers. Every game, Steph and Klay would rain down three-pointers on opponents, setting the stage for the dominance that would take place the following season.

In the 2013–2014 season, Steph led the NBA in three-pointers again and was averaging numbers like 23 points a game and his new high in assists, 8.5. He was making buckets and passing the rock, and if you're scoring AND passing, you're a lethal combination. That year, he earned his first All-Star selection and was named to the All-NBA team. Think of it like being on the honor roll. Despite the team having the fourth-best defense in the league and finishing with 51 wins, the most they had since 1992, they once again ended their journey early in the playoffs with a loss to the Los Angeles Clippers. But the front office knew they were on the cusp of something special. A team that was on the rise led by a player who could be unstoppable with the right system and supporting cast. All it would take to get over the hump was a phone call to a fiery player who once played with the GOAT—the Greatest Of All Time—and knew what it took to win multiple championships.

Origin of the
"Splash Brothers"

In 2012, Steph and Klay were dropping threes like nobody's business. On December 21 of that year, during a game against the Charlotte Bobcats, Warriors writer Brian Witt used the hashtag #SplashBrothers on the team's official Twitter account after Steph and Klay had 25 points and seven three-pointers by halftime. Witt was making a reference to another famous Bay Area duo: **Mark McGwire and José Canseco** of the Oakland Athletics, who, due to their towering home runs and slugging power each game, were known as the "Bash Brothers." Pairing that with the fact that any ball Steph or Klay touched seemed to "splash" right through the net, a nickname was born. Steph and Klay together have the most career three-pointers made in history by a duo (6,228); most career three-pointers made in NBA playoff history by a duo (1,119); most career three-pointers made in NBA finals history by a duo (258); and the most three-pointers made in a season by a duo (678), which broke the previous record of 525 set by—you guessed it—Steph Curry and Klay Thompson.

CHAPTER

4

CHAMPIONS

A NEW COACH

When the 2013–2014 season ended, Golden State General Manager Bob Myers knew the Warriors needed more than grit and determination from their talented roster—they needed a new leader. In 2014, the Warriors hired **Steve Kerr** as the 25th head coach in franchise history.

Despite his winning resume as a player, Kerr had never been a head coach before, but he had a clear vision of what the Warriors could become. He envisioned a team that played at a breakneck pace, wearing their opponents out with full-court theatrics and constantly moving the ball to disorient defenses. Kerr was one of history's most proficient three-point shooters himself, so it was fitting that his team would put the longball as their priority. The Golden State Warriors were going to make the three-point shot the most important weapon in the league.

FUN FACTS: Steve Kerr

- Steve was born in Beirut, Lebanon, on September 27, 1965. Much of his childhood was spent in the Middle East, where his father was a university professor.
- He attended the University of Arizona, where he was a standout player for the Wildcats and set an NCAA record for three-point shooting accuracy.
- Kerr has won nine total NBA championships, five as a player and four as a coach (with Golden State).
- Kerr is the only NBA player (since 1969) to win four straight NBA titles from 1996 to 1999.
- Steve is a huge soccer fan and avid supporter of Liverpool F.C.

9 RINGS

Kerr's approach was inspired by a mixture of his time with the Bulls and the San Antonio Spurs where the name of the game was unselfish play. He wanted his team to share the ball, make quick decisions, and always look for the best shot. Steph was at the helm of this offense as point guard and was the perfect person to bring it to life. The Splash Brothers were now fully unleashed, and Steph and Klay weren't just taking three-pointers every now and then, they were making them at an unprecedented rate, leading the league in three-point percentage, assists, and points per game. One thing Kerr stressed was the mantra that they could score all the points in the world, but they still needed to stop the other team. That meant they had to have defense almost as good as their offense. Kerr wanted his team to be well-rounded because if they could do well on defense, they would be unstoppable.

The linchpin of the Warriors defense was **Draymond Green**, a tenacious player with a versatile skillset. Draymond has become known for his short temper, often letting his emotions get the best of him, but for the beginning of this new era, his ferociousness against opposing teams fired up his teammates and helped them win.

THE ROAD TO
GLORY

From the very first game of the 2014–2015 season, it was clear the Warriors were going to be something special. By the middle of the season, Golden State had the best record in the NBA. They weren't just winning— they were dominating.

Meanwhile, Steph was revolutionizing the position. He became almost unguardable, had the quickest release in the league, and would shoot off the dribble, shoot while double or triple guarded, and shoot far behind the three-point line in no-man's land. Defenders started guarding him from the moment he crossed half-court, and at times, even gave him a full court press! But it didn't matter. Steph would find a way to get his shot off and, more often than not, it would go in. That season, he made 286 three-pointers, setting a new NBA record.

100

On March 2, 1962, Wilt Chamberlain scored 100 points in a game against the New York Knicks, an unmatched performance in basketball history. The list below showcases the top-five highest scoring performances in NBA history. See any repeats?

1. 1962: **Wilt Chamberlain** - 100 points
2. 2006: **Kobe Bryant** - 81 points
3. 1961: **Wilt Chamberlain** - 78 points
4. 962: **Wilt Chamberlain** - 73 points
5. 1962: **Wilt Chamberlain** - 73 points

But Steph's brilliance wasn't limited to scoring. When he had the ball, he found his teammates with dazzling passes and elevated everyone around him. Klay was his partner in the backcourt, providing deadly shooting and lockdowns on defense. And with support from Draymond Green, Andre Iguodala, Harrison Barnes, and Andrew Bogut, this was a talented but balanced team that wasn't afraid of anyone. The Warriors finished their season with only 15 losses, a huge improvement since Steph was drafted in 2009. They finished 67–15, the best in the league and the most wins in franchise history. Steph was named the league's MVP, and his hard work—battling through injury, working with multiple coaches and teammates, and dealing with doubters—proved that he was the best player in the league.

That season's playoff run felt different for Steph, as he and his teammates played with a newfound sense of confidence. Their fast-paced offense continued to overwhelm even the best of teams and their defense, anchored by Draymond Green, suffocated every opponent.

The Warriors had made the NBA Finals, their chance to bring a trophy back to the Bay Area. But someone was standing in their way: LeBron James. One of the greatest players of all time was on a mission to bring Cleveland their first basketball championship . . . ever. As always, he was playing like a man possessed, willing to push his body to the limits for the city and its fans.

DURING THIS SERIES,

LeBron James became the first player in NBA Finals history to lead both teams in points, rebounds, and assists for an entire series, averaging 35.8 points, 13.3 rebounds, and 8.7 assists per game.

It was a matter of fate that Steph and LeBron would be going head-to-head in the biggest series of their lives. As you now know, they were born in the same hospital and later crossed paths when LeBron cheered Steph on from the seats of Ford Field in Detroit. But now they were competitors, trying desperately to win for their cities.

The Cavaliers put up a great fight, but they were no match for the Warriors' relentless pacing and small-ball firepower. With Cleveland leading two games to one, the Warriors turned it on. Steph and his teammates hit a then-record of 67 three-pointers in the series, with Steph making 25 of those. In six games, the Warriors clinched their first NBA championship in 40 years. And Steph Curry, the baby-faced assassin with glass ankles who many doubted would ever be more than a fringe player was now a star, an MVP, and a world champion.

THE
RECORD

The NBA Champion Warriors had no time to rest on their laurels after winning the big game. Behind closed doors, teams were no doubt hiring defensive gurus to come up with a formula to stop the Splash Brothers and their merry band of superstars. Meanwhile, the Warriors embraced the challenge and set their sets higher. How high? To become the greatest team in NBA history.

From the start of the 2015–2016 season, Steph and the team played with an unmatched level of intensity and focus. Steph was playing even better than his MVP season, and by the All-Star break, the Warriors had lost only four games. Fans, media, and the NBA world began to ask if the Golden State Warriors could break the record for the most wins in a single season (72-10) set by the 1995–1996 Chicago Bulls. If anyone knew what it was like to achieve that record, it would Steph's coach, Steve Kerr, who had been part of that Bulls team.

72 WINS

10 LOSSES

1995–1996

Steph continued to shatter records, including his own of the most three-pointers made in a season. He hit 402 that year. His teammates also showed up, with Draymond Green recording 13 triple-doubles and Klay Thompson once scoring 37 points in a single quarter. Plus, the Warriors' bench provided ample support. On April 13, 2016, the Warriors defeated the Memphis Grizzlies and secured their 73rd win, breaking the longstanding Bulls record. Steph was rewarded with another MVP honor, the first player in history to win the award unanimously. He received all 131 first-place votes. LeBron James and Shaquille O'Neal almost achieved this accolade, but they were each one vote shy in their respective years.

3–1

During the playoffs, the Warriors made quick work of their opponents on their way to the Finals, but Steph sprained his MCL (one of the ligaments that attaches your thigh bone to your shin bone) in a game against the Houston Rockets. Waiting for the Warriors in the NBA Finals once again was Steph's old friendly foe, LeBron James and the Cleveland Cavaliers. The Warriors got out to an early 3–1 series lead, but then the Cavaliers staged one of the greatest comebacks in NBA history. LeBron James and Kyrie Irving delivered historic performances, becoming the first teammates to each score 40 points in a Finals game. Key injuries to the Warriors, including Steph's lingering MCL issue and Green's suspension for Game 5, shifted the momentum. The Cavaliers' defense tightened, and James' all-around dominance—culminating in a triple-double in Game 7—sealed their victory. The Cavaliers won 93–89, becoming the first team in NBA Finals history to overcome a 3–1 deficit, delivering Cleveland its first championship.

The Warriors weren't sure if they would ever rise again, but a familiar face would answer that question during the summer of 2016, when **Kevin Durant**, one of the best players in the league and another face from Steph's childhood, signed with the team. His deal was met with mixed reactions among fans, with some saying it wasn't fair he was joining an already stacked team. But the Warriors, and Steph, were thrilled. Their starting lineup—Curry, Thompson, Green, and

Durant—were all All-Stars. Durant, a big player who could shoot from anywhere, fit in seamlessly on the 2016–2017 squad. Once again, the team was virtually unstoppable, finishing with a 67–15 record and the top seed in the playoffs.

KEVIN DURANT is one of the most dominant and versatile players in NBA history, known for his scoring, agility, and impressive wingspan. He stands 6 feet, 10 inches with a 7-foot, 5-inch wingspan!

7'-5"

6'-10"

In the playoffs that season, the Warriors kept racking up firsts. They became the first team in NBA history to start the playoffs 12–0. Then they reached the NBA Finals, and we'll give you one guess as to who was waiting for them—*again*. The Cleveland Cavaliers were back for the third consecutive year, but this time around, there was no miraculous comeback. The Cavs had no answer for the addition of Durant. The Warriors easily won the series in five games.

The following year, the 2017–2018 Warriors didn't take their foot off the gas, and for the final time, they met LeBron James and the Cavaliers in the Finals and swept them again. The Warriors were on top of the world—but sometimes the best things can't last. With their incredible run beset by many challenges including injuries, fatigue, and the mounting pressure of maintaining greatness, Kevin Durant decided that he wanted another challenge and left the team in 2019.

But true champions never stay down for long. For the next few years, it wouldn't be easy for the Warriors, but with Steve Kerr staying at the helm and Steph Curry still captain, the Warriors were determined to reclaim their throne.

In the 2021–2022 season, the Warriors had missed the playoffs two years in a row, but Steph didn't give up. He posted great numbers for the regular season, with 25.5 points per game, and broke the NBA's all-time three-point-record at Madison Square Garden. After securing the third seed in the playoffs, the Warriors were able to dispatch the Denver Nuggets, Memphis Grizzlies, and Dallas Mavericks to return to the NBA Finals. This time, the Boston Celtics were waiting, led by exciting young talents Jayson Tatum and Jaylen Brown. Each game in that finals series was a tough-fought battle with high drama and amazing performances, including from Steph in Game 4 when he scored 43 points to win the game and even the series. Led by Steph's determination, the Warriors claimed their fourth championship in eight years. For the first time in his career, Steph was named Finals MVP, finally silencing any haters who said he couldn't lead his team to victory once again.

AN OLYMPIC DREAM
COME TRUE

For many years, despite having a packed trophy case along with his Hall of Fame resume, there was one elusive accolade that Steph wanted: an Olympic gold medal. Unfortunately, injuries, fatigue, and other factors had kept him from participating in the Olympics until Paris 2024 was around the corner. Steph was 36 years old and knew it might be his last chance at getting a medal.

! TOTALLY AWESOME FACTS !
The Summer Olympics

- The Olympic Games date back to 776 BCE in Ancient Greece, with the first events including running, long jump, and javelin. Instead of gold medals, winners were awarded olive-leaf crowns.

- The first modern Olympics took place in Athens, Greece, in 1896. The first athlete to ever win a gold medal was James Connolly from the United States, who won the triple jump.

- Did you know the Olympic symbol of five interlocking rings represents unity? They are colored blue, yellow, black, green, and red because every national flag in the world contains at least one of those colors.

- The most decorated Olympian ever is swimmer Michael Phelps, who has 28 medals—23 of them gold! The US has nearly 3,000 Summer Olympics medals total, making them the country with the most overall.

- Women first competed in the Olympics in 1900, in Paris, in only a small number of events. Now, women compete in almost every sport and make up almost half of all Olympians.

Once Steph committed to representing his country, it became an even more meaningful opportunity as he had the chance to play alongside LeBron James for the first time in real competition. Steph also got to re-team with his once-championship teammate, Kevin Durant. But even with the Curry, James, and Durant power trio, the journey toward a gold medal was anything but easy for Team USA. In the semifinal game, Serbia gave them trouble, with Team USA only winning by four points. Then came the finals, when the US would play the French team in their home country, in a stadium full of their own fans.

The gold medal game between Team USA and Team France took place on Saturday, August 10, 2024. Team USA held the lead for most of the game, but the passionate home crowd inspired the French team to keep the game close. When the US lead shrunk to just three points, Steph became possessed by his alter ego, "Chef Curry" (a nickname given to him for the way he "cooks" his opponents on the court). With his confidence unlocked, nothing was going to stop Steph from winning that gold medal, even if he had to take the hardest shots of his career to do it.

WHAT FUELS YOU

when you participate in any sort of competition? Is it the chance of winning, the fun of playing, or having the chance to improve your skills?

In the final 2 minutes and 47 seconds of the tense game, Steph Curry drained *four* three-pointers, each one more amazing than the last. In fact, all 24 points that Steph Curry had in the game were from three-pointers. But it was the final shot, the "Golden Dagger" as the announcers called it, that sealed the game. With 43 seconds left, Steph was being double-teamed and passed the ball to his old friend Kevin Durant. Steph managed to get open again, got the ball, did a few ball-handling marvels with a behind-the-back crossover, and in the face of two players jumping at him, with 36 seconds left, took his shot. *Splash*. Game over. Steph, and many of his teammates (including LeBron) did his signature "Night Night" gesture, with his hands on the side of his face. For Steph, the moment would go down as one of the highlights of his career. For the first and last time, he was able to compete in the greatest games in the world, and he helped his team—and his country—bring home the gold medal.

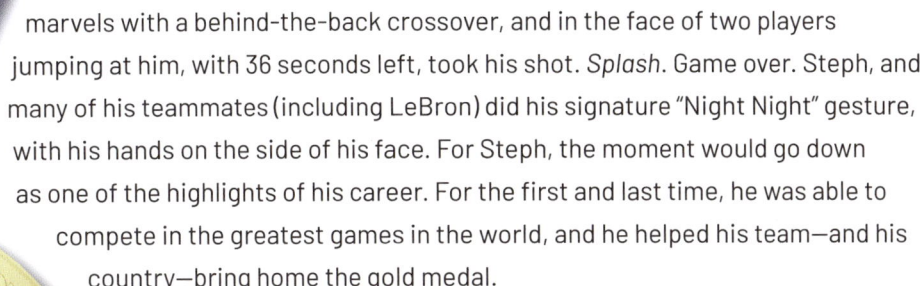

AFTER WINNING GOLD, Steph celebrated in style, wearing a hoodie with "Nuit Nuit" on the chest (French for "Night Night"). His game-winning performance inspired several memes, like McDonald's France jokingly considering removing their "Spicy Curry" sauce in response to the defeat.

CHAPTER

OFF THE COURT

GIVING
BACK

Steph has built an important and impactful legacy in business, philanthropy, and popular culture. He's used his massive platform to influence the world positively and has given back to his fans, his community, and those in need.

But Steph would probably agree that his most important job in the world is being a father, a husband, and a dedicated family man. He's been married to **Ayesha Curry** since 2011, and they have four children: **Riley**, **Ryan**, Canon, and Caius. While Steph was on the court, Ayesha started her own empire with multiple businesses as an entrepreneur, helped run organizations with Steph, and became a popular chef with her own cookbooks. But the biggest star in the Curry family might be Riley Curry, who, when she was just two years old during the 2015 NBA Finals, joined her dad at the podium during his press conference. Riley's antics captured the hearts of millions, especially when she told her dad to be quiet because she thought he was talking too much. The moment went viral, and we all got to see a different side of Steph.

GOLF

Steph has been playing golf since he was 10 years old. In 2023, he won the American Century Championship, a prestigious celebrity tournament, and made headlines by sinking a hole-in-one on a 152-yard par-3 seventh hole—an amazing feat!

Here are some other golf facts you might not know:

- Golf is one of the oldest sports in the world. Ancient Romans played a game with a ball made of feathers, and the Chinese had a similar game involving a ball with a target, but golf as we know it was started in Scotland in the fifteenth century, with the first recorded game taking place over 500 years ago, in 1457.

- Why does a typical golf course have 18 holes? In 1764, at the Old Course at St. Andrews, Scotland, the course had 22 holes, but after they deemed two of the holes too short, they combined four holes into two and got 18. The number stuck!

- We've all seen a golf ball, but did you know they used to be made with leather and stuffed with feathers? Until the mid-nineteenth century, when rubber balls were the norm, these feather-filled balls, called "featheries," were the standard.

- Golf is the only universal sport—literally. In 1971, astronaut Alan Shepard, as part of the Apollo 14 mission, hit two golf balls on the moon. This makes golf the first and only sport to be played on the moon.

- There are almost 40,000 golf courses in the world, with 17,000 of those in the United States.

Steph's underdog mentality, shaped by years of being overlooked and labeled "too weak" to succeed at the highest levels, inspired him to create Underrated, a brand that celebrates kids like him who were underestimated and had to fight for recognition. He also realized that athletes in his former position lacked an outlet to showcase their talent and potential, so he launched the **Underrated** camp specifically for high school players who, like him, didn't have national attention or high rankings. The camp gives under-the-radar players a chance to shine and gain exposure to coaches, scouts, and opportunities that otherwise would have been out of reach. The camp was a huge success and allowed him to also launch Underrated Golf, which recognized the severe lack of diversity in the sport and creates opportunities for athletes in marginalized communities who are interested in learning more about golf, a game he is extremely passionate about.

In 2018, Steph cofounded Unanimous Media, a production company that focuses on developing, creating, and distributing compelling family, faith, and sports content. The company is named Unanimous after Steph's historic MVP award in 2016. Unanimous Media helped make *The Queen of Basketball*, a documentary short film about sports pioneer Lucia Stewart (who was the first woman drafted in the NBA). Steph won an Academy Award for producing the film. Unanimous even made a documentary about Steph and his life called *Underrated* on Apple TV+.

IF SOMEONE MADE

a movie about your life, who would you cast to play you and why?

Steph is also a published author. He's written three children's books (*I Have a Superpower*, *I Am Extraordinary*, and *Sports Superheroes*), all of which empower readers to embrace their differences and follow their dreams.

But the one area that makes Steph the proudest is his work with charity. His philanthropic efforts are driven by his passion to give back and make a difference in the world. All his causes focus on helping children, fighting hunger, and advocating for social justice, so everyone gets a fair shake in this world.

IN NOVEMBER 2024,

Steph spoiled former Splash Brother Klay Thompson's Bay Area homecoming by beating his Dallas Mavericks. At 36 years old, Steph made history by becoming the oldest point guard to record back-to-back 30-point games. He also joined LeBron James and Michael Jordan as the only players 36 years old or older with consecutive 35-point games.

In 2012, Steph became involved with the United Nations Foundation's Nothing but Nets campaign (now known as United to Beat Malaria), which was a grassroots campaign to raise awareness and fight malaria. The original campaign was inspired by Rick Reilly, a *Sports Illustrated* writer who challenged readers to donate $10 to purchase anti-malaria bed nets. In order to help, Steph not only donated money but was able to use his skills on the court to create change in the world. For every three-pointer he made during the NBA season, he donated three insecticide-treated mosquito nets to combat malaria. These nets help prevent mosquitoes from biting people while they sleep, which helps stop the spread of the disease. This was the first time Steph realized he could use his image and popularity to help people in a tangible way.

When Nothing but Nets gained public attention and raised a lot of funds, Steph got an invite from none other than **President Barack Obama** to speak at the White House. This was the start of Steph's friendship with President Obama, who has been a big supporter—despite being a die-hard Chicago Bulls fan.

This early work in Steph's career helped prepare him for his biggest project yet, one that he would start with his wife Ayesha and that would bring them closer than ever to their adopted home of Oakland, California. In 2019, the couple started **Eat. Learn. Play.**, an amazing foundation that helps kids unlock their full potential. The foundation focuses on three important areas for kids: Eat (nutrition), Learn (literacy), and Play (physical activity). The organization has provided over six million healthy school meals annually to almost 35,000 students in Oakland. They even have a mobile resource center, known as the Eat. Learn. Play. Bus, to deliver nutritious meals and books to families in need. When it comes to education, the organization has invested a lot of money in literacy initiatives that help fund classroom projects. They've also enhanced school sports programs and remodeled schoolyards to create safe spaces to play. In 2023, the Currys announced they were raising and investing $50 million to support students in Oakland so they could have the resources they need to thrive.

Hey There,

Changemaker!

You don't have to be a millionaire or billionaire to be a philanthropist! Philanthropy is for anyone who wants to help others. Have you ever thought about how you could make the world a better place? Here are some charities you can get involved with to help you make a difference like Steph Curry:

- **UNICEF Kid Power (gokidpower.org):** You can help malnourished kids around the world by completing challenges. The more active you are, the more food and support UNICEF will send to children in need.

- **DoSomething.org:** Join online campaigns to tackle major issues by doing things like making blankets for homeless shelters or creating anti-bullying posters for school.

- **Free Rice (freerice.com):** Fight world hunger by playing vocabulary games. Each correct answer donates rice to people in need.

- **Local Animal Shelters:** Volunteer to walk dogs, play with cats, or make toys for shelter animals. Find a local shelter at www.adoptapet.com to get involved.

- **Little Free Library:** Start a mini library in your neighborhood or donate old books to one near you. Your old books could change someone's life. Check out littlefreelibrary.org for more information.

GLOBAL IMPACT
AND LEGACY

Steph may seem like just a basketball player, but to millions of fans across the world, he's an icon. He once received a letter from a nine-year-old superfan named Riley Morrison, who noticed that Steph's Curry 5 sneakers were only available in boys' and men's sizes. Her heartfelt letter said that girls wanted to rock the Curry 5s too and that it wasn't fair how they were labeled. Steph, who has long been an advocate for gender equality, was moved by the letter and quickly got Under Armour to fix the problem by making all shoes unisex and listing both men's and women's sizes. Steph even invited Riley to help design a special edition of the shoes with her artwork and honored her at the Golden State Warriors game on International Women's Day. Take that as a powerful reminder that no one is too young to make a difference or inspire change.

When it comes to the NBA, Steph Curry transformed the sport of basketball. The game didn't evolve *with* Steph, it evolved *because* of Steph. His stats, accolades, style of play, and versatility have influenced basketball globally, but Steph wants his legacy to transcend his achievements on the court. When you combine his NBA career, the ways he's given back, and the type of person he is, his legacy may seem like it's already finished. But in true Steph fashion, if the game ain't over, that means he's only getting started.

THE WHITE HOUSE
WASHINGTON

WHAT DO YOU

want to be remembered for someday? Is there a talent or accomplishment that you would like to be known and celebrated for?

CHAPTER

OVERTIME

BUILD YOUR OWN
SUPER TEAM

Over the course of NBA history, several franchises have had what is called a super team, a collection of stellar players (who are clearly future Hall of Fame candidates or All-Pro players) who team up like the Avengers to dominate the league. In the past decade, it's become the norm for players to jump around from team to team to find the best super team in the hope of winning a championship and dominating the league.

Famous Super Teams
in the NBA

★ The 1980s Los Angeles Lakers (known as the "Showtime Lakers"), featuring Magic Johnson, Kareem Abdul-Jabbar, James Worthy, Byron Scott, and Michael Cooper

★ The 1980s Boston Celtics, featuring Larry Bird, Kevin McHale, Robert Parish, Dennis Johnson, and Danny Ainge

★ The 2007-2012 Boston Celtics, featuring Kevin Garnett, Paul Pierce, Ray Allen, and Rajon Rondo

★ The 2010-2014 Miami Heat, featuring LeBron James, Dwayne Wade, Chris Bosh, and Ray Allen

★ The 2016-2019 Golden State Warriors, featuring Steph Curry, Klay Thompson, Draymond Green, and Kevin Durant

STEPH CURRY'S FANTASY ALL-TIME STARTING 5

POINT GUARD

Magic Johnson

SHOOTING GUARD

Michael Jordan

POWER FORWARD

Tim Duncan

SMALL FORWARD

Kobe Bryant

CENTER

Shaquille O'Neal

During a puppy interview for BuzzFeed in 2023 (an interview where you answer questions while playing with adorable puppies), Steph Curry was asked about his all-time starting five rotation. Always the humble legend, Curry refrained from putting himself on the team (despite the team clearly needing some help with distance shooting) or any of his peers currently in the NBA (*cough* LeBron James *cough*).

Curry's formidable team is composed of legends from NBA history with a combined 25 NBA championships and 12 MVP awards. Talk about firepower!

Now it's time for you to imagine yourself as the general manager of your very own NBA dream team—but there's a catch! Your salary cap is $15. You might be asking yourself, "How can anyone build an NBA team for $15?" Well, you'll be using a special grid featuring different basketball stars (all stars who have retired, like Steph chose) where each player has a price tag. The best players cost $5, while others will be more of a bargain. Your job as general manager is to choose one player from each position without going over your budget. Once you're done, compare your super team to your friends' teams and try to figure out who would win in a game or a best of seven championship series.

YOUR DREAM TEAM

	PG POINT GUARD	SG SHOOTING GUARD	SF SMALL FORWARD	PF POWER FORWARD	C CENTER
$5	MAGIC JOHNSON	MICHAEL JORDAN	LARRY BIRD	TIM DUNCAN	KAREEM ABDUL-JABBAR
$4	JOHN STOCKTON	KOBE BRYANT	JULIUS ERVING	KARL MALONE	BILL RUSSELL
$3	ISIAH THOMAS	JOHN STARKS	SCOTTIE PIPPEN	KEVIN GARNETT	SHAQUILLE O'NEAL
$2	OSCAR ROBERTSON	ALLEN IVERSON	DOMINIQUE WILKINS	DIRK NOWITZKI	WILT CHAMBERLAIN
$1	STEVE NASH	REGGIE MILLER	PAUL PIERCE	CHARLES BARKLEY	HAKEEM OLAJUWON

Owner vs. General Manager vs. Head Coach
Who's Really in Charge?

The Head Coach, General Manager, and Owner play a crucial role in a team's success and must work together to put their team in the best position to win. The hierarchy of an NBA team starts with the Owner, who hires the General Manager, who hires the Head Coach.

OWNER

A team's ultimate decision-maker. Not only do they provide the money to back the team, but they are also in charge of setting the overall vision or goals for the franchise and making all the major business decisions. They usually stay out of day-to-day operations but often influence major choices like hiring a General Manager (GM) or approving major trades. Some teams, like the Chicago Bulls, Detroit Pistons, and Los Angeles Clippers, have a single owner, while others are owned by many people or by investment groups.

GENERAL MANAGER

Oversees all the team's operations, which can include acquiring new players, trading players, and getting draft picks. They are in charge of the scouting team that is used to evaluate talent, they negotiate contracts, and build a roster while staying within the salary cap constraints (much like you're doing with the grid right now!). The GM is also the person who hires and fires coaches and other staff members (usually with blessing from the owners).

HEAD COACH

Works closely with all the players and instills their own basketball philosophy and scheme to improve the team and build chemistry among the players. They lead practices, design plays, manage rotations and substitutions during a game, and with their team of assistant coaches, formulate game plans and directions for the team. On top of overseeing the on-court strategy, development of the players, and all game-day decisions, the coach is the most visible member of the administration and in some cases (like with Phil Jackson, George Popovich, Pat Riley, and Steve Kerr) can become a star of the team in their own right.

THE
GOAT GAME

What does it mean to be the GOAT? Not that horned and hoofed animal that scales mountains, is known for its scraggly beard, and produces milk that makes several cheeses—we're talking about the Greatest Of All Time.

Thanks to his dazzling shots from unimaginable angles and lengths on the court (that can hardly be guarded), Steph Curry is widely known as the greatest shooter the NBA has ever seen. But does that make him the GOAT of the NBA? Probably not. At least not yet. That term is usually reserved for Michael Jordan. Or maybe you think it should be LeBron James? There's no right or wrong answer in a GOAT debate. It's a chance to share what you love about your favorite things, open your mind to new perspectives, ideas, and facts, and learn why others love who and what they love.

You'll find a few potential GOAT debate prompts on the next page to get the ball rolling. Each prompt has some helpful examples, but remember, you know your favorites, so argue for them passionately and respectfully. When considering the GOAT in any field, look at things like achievements and records, how long someone has been around, popularity, and your own personal preference.

WHO OR WHAT IS THE GOAT OF . . . ?

NBA Logos
❑ Chicago Bulls ❑ Los Angeles Lakers
❑ Boston Celtics ❑ Toronto Raptors
❑ Miami Heat

Sports Video Game Franchises
❑ Madden ❑ NBA 2K ❑ FIFA
❑ Tony Hawk's Pro Skater
❑ Gran Turismo

THE CHICAGO BULLS are the only NBA team that has never changed their logo. If you could change any of the NBA logos to something different (style, colors, design), what would it be?

NBA Players
❑ Michael Jordan ❑ LeBron James
❑ Bill Russell ❑ Steph Curry
❑ Kobe Bryant

NFL Quarterbacks
❑ Tom Brady ❑ Peyton Manning
❑ Patrick Mahomes ❑ Joe Montana
❑ John Elway

Soccer Players
❑ Lionel Messi ❑ Christiano Ronaldo
❑ Pelé ❑ Diego Maradona
❑ David Beckham

NHL Players
❑ Wayne Gretzky ❑ Mario Lemieux
❑ Gordy Howe ❑ Jaromir Jagr
❑ Martin Brodeur

Olympic Athletes
❑ Michael Phelps
❑ Usain Bolt
❑ Simone Biles ❑ Carl Lewis
❑ Katie Ledecky

Tennis Players
❑ Roger Federer ❑ **Serena Williams** ❑ Rafael Nadal
❑ Novak Djokovic
❑ Steffi Graf

MLB Players
❑ Babe Ruth ❑ Shohei Ohtani ❑ Willie Mays
❑ Hank Aaron ❑ Bryce Harper

FULL COURT FACTS

INSIDE THE WORLD OF STEPH CURRY

You've seen him sink impossible shots. You've watched him dribble circles around the league's toughest defenders. And you've seen him lead the Golden State Warriors to victory time and time again. But do you really know Stephen Curry? Get ready to dive into the awesome, surprising, and cool world of one of the Splash Brothers himself.

! TOTALLY AWESOME FACTS !
The Rubik's Cube

1. Originally called the Magic Cube, the Rubik's Cube was invented in 1974 by Hungarian architect Ernő Rubik.

2. With six sides, containing nine color stickers (orange, yellow, green, red, white, and blue), there are 43 quintillion possible configurations of a Rubik's Cube. If you took one Rubik's Cube for every possible configuration, you could cover the Earth 275 times or stack them on top of each other and reach 261 light-years high.

3. Despite the number of configurations, you can solve the cube with just 20 moves.

4. The fastest solve of a Rubik's Cube was recorded in 2023 by speedcuber Max Park, who solved the puzzle in 3.13 seconds.

Eye Color

Steph has green eyes and was often called "the green-eyed monster" by his mother, Sonya.

Astrological Sign

Pisces

Steph Curry: The Movie

If Steph could choose an actor to play him in a movie it would be Denzel Washington, with Jamie Foxx as a close second.

Favorite Movies

Wedding Crashers, *A Walk to Remember*, and *The Princess Diaries*. He can quote the last two word-for-word after seeing them hundreds of times alongside his sister, Sydel.

Biggest Fear

Ophidiophobia, aka fear of snakes. Who would have thought Steph and Indiana Jones had the same fear!

Hidden Talent

Solving a Rubik's Cube and the ability to juggle.

Favorite Sports Teams Growing Up

Boston Red Sox, Charlotte Hornets, and Carolina Panthers.

Favorite Warriors Jersey Design

Black jerseys with THE TOWN on the front.

DO YOU HAVE

a favorite movie or television show that you would absolutely love to star in?

Favorite Internet Video

"Grape Lady falls"

Off-the-Court Outfit

Hoodie with shorts, jeans, or sweatpants. Steph says, "Every season is hoodie season."

Popcorn Fanatic

In 2019, Steph ranked the popcorn at every NBA arena on a 1-to-5-point scale in the criteria of freshness, saltiness, crunchiness, butter, and presentation. The top-five best arenas were:

5. Sacramento Kings
4. Portland Trail Blazers
3. Miami Heat
2. Brooklyn Nets
1. Dallas Mavericks.

The worst popcorn in the league? The LA Clippers/Los Angeles Lakers.

Fast Food Order

Chick-fil-A spicy chicken sandwich and French fries with extra Chick-fil-A and Polynesian sauce and a lemonade.

Shoe Size

Steph wears size 12½ and sometimes 13, based on the shoe.

Famous Friends

The first person to call Steph after he won the 2022 NBA Championship was friend (and former president) Barack Obama.

THE BIGGEST FEET

in NBA history belong to none other than Shaquille O'Neal, who started his career at size 20. His feet eventually reached their final size of 22!

Nickname Origin

The nickname Chef Curry comes from a Drake lyric from "0 to 100 / The Catch Up," referencing Curry constantly cooking (or scoring) on the court. Steph admits the real chef in the family is his wife, Ayesha.

Trading Places

If Steph could trade places with any athlete, *Freaky Friday*–style, it would be with golfer Rory McIlroy. Curry is an avid golfer that some believe has the tools to become a pro if he wanted to.

⚡ SPOTLIGHT ⚡
Rory McIlroy

Rory McIlroy, born in Northern Ireland, is one of the best golfers in the world and is considered one of the best of his generation. At age 16, McIlroy dropped out of high school to pursue his golf dreams, with his parents' permission. Like Steph Curry, McIlroy is known for his smaller stature, but he is also one of the longest drivers. He has been ranked No. 1 in the world for over 100 weeks and is one of only three golfers in history to win four major championships before the age of 25. In 2022, McIlroy, along with Tiger Woods, started a new golf league, TGL (Tomorrow's Golf League), in partnership with the PGA. One of its initial investors was Steph Curry.

A SPLASH OF
EXCELLENCE

In just 15 years in the NBA, Steph Curry has amassed a gigantic collection of trophies, awards, and record-breaking moments. Much like Steph when he's on a hot streak from beyond the arc (and simply can't miss), his accomplishments just keep piling up. These are just some of the highlights from Steph's career, both on and off the court. (Because if we tried to put all his records and awards in one place, it would be as long as this book!)

HAVE YOU ever won an award for something? Is there one award you would love to win one day?

NCAA

- Men's NCAA single-season record for three-pointers made (2008): 162*
- NCAA Scoring Leader (2008–2009): 28.6 points per game
- SoCon Player of the Year: 2008, 2009

- Davidson College All-Time Leading Scorer (2,635 points, in just three seasons)
- AP All-American

*Caitlin Clark (University of Iowa) holds the all-time record (men's or women's) for most three-pointers in a single NCAA season (2023) with 201.

NBA ACCOLADES

(as of the end of the 2023–2024 season)

- 4× NBA Champion (2015, 2017, 2018, 2022)
- 2× NBA MVP (2015, 2016)
- 1× NBA Finals MVP (2022)
- 2× NBA Scoring Leader (2016, 2021)
- 7× NBA three-point field goals leader (2013, 2014, 2015, 2016, 2017, 2021, 2022)
- 10× All-Star (2014, 2015, 2016, 2017, 2018, 2019, 2021, 2022, 2023, 2024)
- 2× All-Star Three-Point Contest Winner (2015, 2021)
- 4× All-NBA First Team (2015, 2016, 2019, 2021)
- 4× All-NBA Second Team (2014, 2017, 2022, 2023)
- Most three-pointers made in a season (402; Steph is also ranked 3, 4, 5, and 6 in the Top 10)
- Most three-pointers made in history (3,747 and counting)
- Most consecutive games with a three-pointer (268)
- Most half-court shots made (6)
- Most Playoff three-pointers made (618)
- Most games with 10+ three-pointers made (25)
- 50-40-90 club (50% field goals, 40% three-pointers, and 90% free throws)
- Highest all-time free throw percentage (90.9%)
- Olympic Gold Medalist (Paris 2024)

Pro Basketball

You've seen LeBron James, Steph Curry, Nikola Jokić, and Jayson Tatum hold it up in the air. It's 2 feet (0.6 m) tall, weighs 15½ pounds (7 kg) and is made of vermeil and sterling silver, with a 24-karat gold overlay by Tiffany & Co. But do you know its name?

The NBA championship trophy is called the Larry O'Brien Trophy, named after former NBA commissioner Lawrence "Larry" O'Brien, who oversaw the league from 1975 to 1984. In that time, he oversaw the merger of the NBA and ABA, expanding the league from 18 teams to 23 (there are now 30), and helped introduce the three-point shot, which would forever be changed by Steph Curry.

Most of the NBA trophies are named after someone, like these:

- **Rookie of the Year: Wilt Chamberlain** Trophy
- **MVP (Most Valuable Player):** Michael Jordan Trophy
- **All-Star Game MVP:** Kobe Bryant Trophy
- **NBA Finals MVP: Bill Russell** Trophy
- **Defensive Player of the Year:** Hakeem Olajuwon Trophy

OFF THE COURT

- **Academy Award (as Executive Producer) for Best Documentary Short Film:** *The Queen of Basketball* (2022)
- *Time* **100 Most Influential People** (2016)
- *Sports Illustrated* **Sportsperson of the year** (2018, 2022)
- **NBA Social Justice Champion Award** (2023)
- **J. Walter Kennedy Citizenship Award** (2023)

- **NBA Community Assist Award** (2014)
- **Jackie Robinson Sports Award** (2021)
- **3× Teen Choice Award** winner (Choice Male Athlete in 2015, 2016, 2017)
- **8× ESPY Award winner** (Best Male Athlete, NBA Player ×3, Record-Breaking Performance ×2, Best Team ×2)

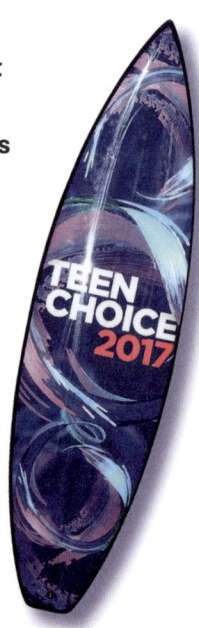

THE ULTIMATE
STEPH CURRY QUIZ

So, you've read the book. That means you should be an expert on all things Steph Curry, right? Let's put it to the test. Below are 10 questions about Steph's life and career, to see how much you learned. Quiz yourself, quiz your friends and family, and after you're done, see who has the best shooting percentage (correct answers)!

 At what point in the 2008 NCAA Division I men's basketball tournament did Curry become a national sensation?

      A. Sweet Sixteen

      B. Elite Eight

      C. Final Four

      D. Finals

 The 2015–2016 Curry-led Warriors went 73-9 to achieve the best regular season in NBA history, beating the previous record of 72-10 by what team?

      A. San Antonio Spurs

      B. Los Angeles Lakers

      C. Chicago Bulls

      D. Boston Celtics

3 Inspired by a famous nickname given to Oakland Athletics sluggers Mark McGwire and José Canseco, Warriors writer Brian Witt gave what now-iconic nickname to Steph Curry and Klay Thompson due to their exciting playing style?

    A. Swish Brothers

    B. Swoosh Brothers

    C. Sink Brothers

    D. Splash Brothers

4 In what city was Steph born? (Remember, it's the same city—and hospital—where his longtime rival LeBron James was also born.)

    A. Akron, Ohio

    B. Columbus, Ohio

    C. Dayton, Ohio

    D. Cleveland, Ohio

5 What famous NBA player (and teammate of his father, Dell Curry) would play one-on-one with a young Steph before every home game in Toronto?

    A. Alonzo Mourning

    B. Vince Carter

    C. Kendall Gill

    D. Larry Johnson

IF YOU could play one-on-one with any player in NBA history, who would it be and why?

6 What clothing brand did Steph have a sponsorship deal with before he ultimately began a successful partnership with Under Armour?

 A. Reebok

 B. Puma

 C. Adidas

 D. Nike

7 What particular on-court habit is Steph known for that he picked up while playing in college?

 A. Wearing mismatched socks for good luck

 B. Kissing his necklace after every logo three

 C. Biting on his mouthguard

 D. Closing his eyes before shooting free throws

8 The world may know him as Steph Curry, but "Steph" is actually his middle name. Do you remember his first name?

 A. Reginald

 B. Wardell

 C. Randell

 D. William

Steph in the Middle

Steph Curry is just one of many famous people who prefer to go by their middle name instead of their first name. Did you know the following notable people *also* use their middle name?

- Rachel **Meghan Markle**
- John **William Ferrell**
- Paul **Kevin Jonas II**
- Robyn **Rihanna Fenty**
- James **Paul McCartney**

9 At the beginning of his career, Steph had a promise with his mom, Sonya, that he would accomplish what feat during his lifetime?

    A. Get a college degree

    B. Win a gold medal

    C. Win an MVP award

    D. Win Sixth Man of the Year

10 Which one of Steph and Ayesha Curry's four children joined Steph during a press conference for the NBA playoffs?

    A. Caius

    B. Ryan

    C. Cannon

    D. Riley

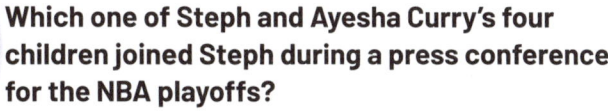

Answers: 1. B, 2. C, 3. D, 4. A, 5. B, 6. D, 7. C, 8. B, 9. A, 10. D

THE HOME COURT

CHALLENGE

SHOOT LIKE STEPH

Have you ever wanted to shoot like Steph Curry? It might seem impossible, but just remember that he didn't start out as the greatest of all time! It took hard work, dedication, and practice. We've compiled some of Steph's favorite techniques to help you start cooking up the court just like Chef Curry.

MECHANICS

Your power comes from your legs, not your arms. When shooting, point your toes in the same direction, squared with the rim. Push the arches of your feet into the floor and keep your knees behind your toes. Let the energy flow from your feet, through your hips and glutes, and through the ball as you release.

Hand placement is critical. Steph likes to place his index finger on the air valve of the ball and holds the ball with his finger pads (leaving space between the ball and his palm) while aiming for the two to three hooks holding the net that face him. He imagines dropping the ball over the hooks. Keep a high release point with your elbow above your eye. That'll make it harder for defenders to block.

DRILLS

Mirror Practice

Stand in front of a mirror with no ball. Focus on feet position, lower body alignment, and finishing your shot with your elbow above your eye.

Always Find the Rim

Spend 10 minutes just walking around the court and locating the rim hooks from different angles. Practice running to spots and miming your shot.

Hand Placement

Practice putting your index finger on the air valve, taking 10 shots with this placement, then 10 more without your palm. Repeat until it's natural.

Close Range

Start a few feet or about one meter from the basket. Use your mechanics. Make 5 perfect shots in a row, tracking your attempts. Step back a little farther after each set.

Expanding Range

Use the chart on the next page (with 12 different spots) to practice. Aim to make 5 from each spot during practice.

Take Notes

Track where you miss shots and adjust your mechanics. Practice running to each spot to take a shot as if you're in a game.

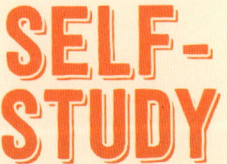

SELF-STUDY

Dell Curry's secret weapon in training Steph was a camera. Set up a camera or your phone on a tripod and film yourself shooting from the front and side. Analyze your form after practice to spot and correct your mistakes.

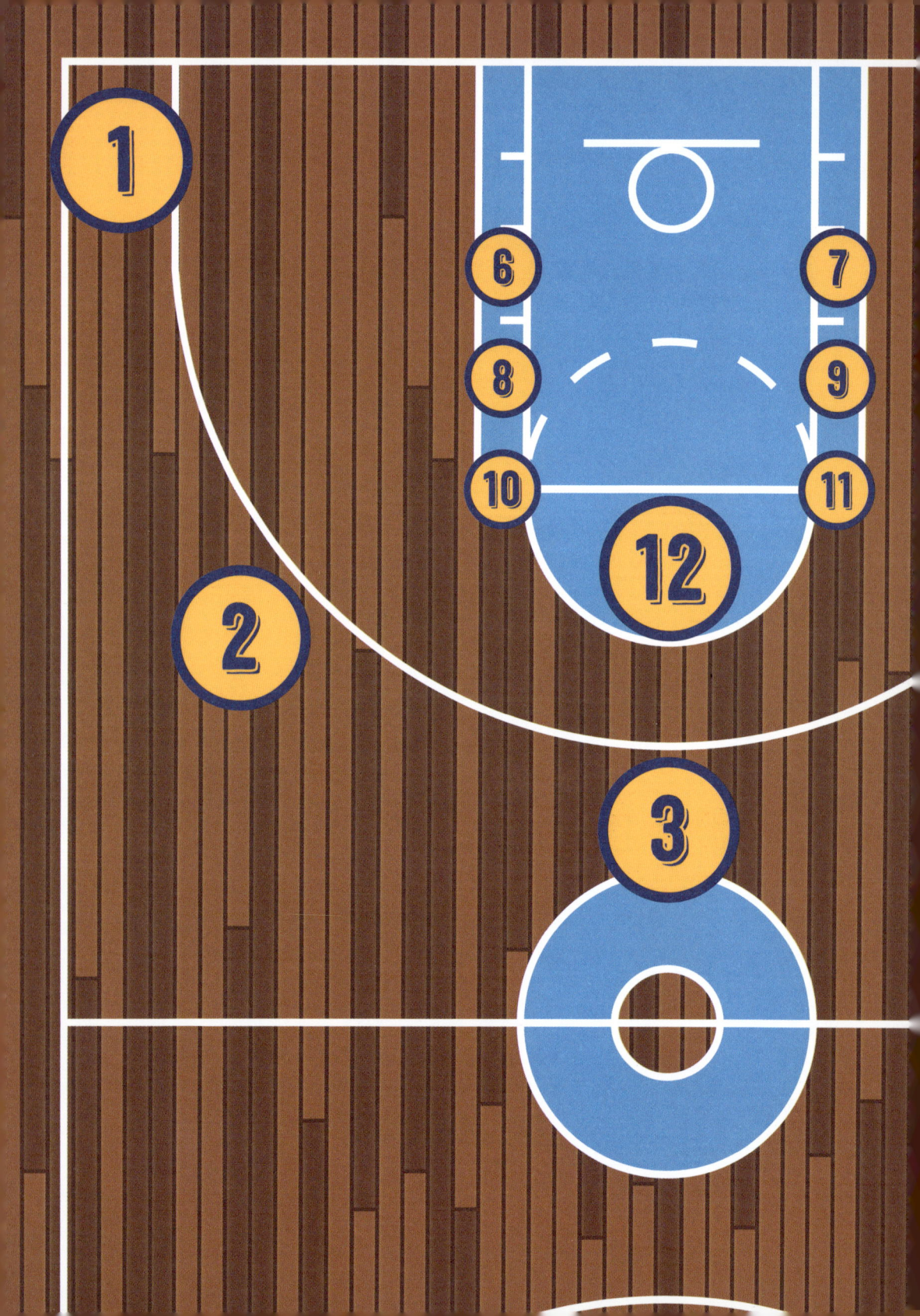

QUICK WORKOUT PLAN

Keep your body in top shape like Steph with these simple exercises. They'll help strengthen your legs and core to improve your shooting.

- **10 jumping jacks**
- **10 squats**
- **30-second plank**

Final Words

Finish all your responsibilities at home and school before you get to work on the court. That means chores and homework are done before you bounce a ball. When you're done practicing, take a moment to visualize getting better. When you're done, be like Steph, and think about one way you can help someone (a friend, family, or stranger) and do that for them. Steph is all about business on the court and helping people off it. If you want to be like Steph, you will be too.

EVERY CHAMPION IN
NBA HISTORY
(1946-2024)

2023-24 | Boston Celtics

2022-23 | Denver Nuggets

2021-22 | Golden State Warriors

2020-21 | Milwaukee Bucks

2019-20 | Los Angeles Lakers

2018-19 | Toronto Raptors

2017-18 | Golden State Warriors

2016-17 | Golden State Warriors

2015-16 | Cleveland Cavaliers

2014-15 | Golden State Warriors

2013-14 | San Antonio Spurs

2012-13 | Miami Heat

2011-12 | Miami Heat

2010-11 | Dallas Mavericks

2009-10 | Los Angeles Lakers

2008-09 | Los Angeles Lakers

2007–08 | Boston Celtics

2006–07 | San Antonio Spurs

2005–06 | Miami Heat

2004–05 | San Antonio Spurs

2003–04 | Detroit Pistons

2002–03 | San Antonio Spurs

2001–02 | Los Angeles Lakers

2000–01 | Los Angeles Lakers

1999–2000 | Los Angeles Lakers

1998–99 | San Antonio Spurs

1997–98 | Chicago Bulls

1996–97 | Chicago Bulls

1995–96 | Chicago Bulls

1994–95 | Houston Rockets

1993–94 | Houston Rockets

1992–93 | Chicago Bulls

1991–92 | Chicago Bulls

1990–91 | Chicago Bulls

1989–90 | Detroit Pistons

1988–89 | Detroit Pistons

1987–88 | Los Angeles Lakers

LeBron James
4 championships

1986-87 | Los Angeles Lakers

1985-86 | Boston Celtics

1984-85 | Los Angeles Lakers

1983-84 | Boston Celtics

1982-83 | Philadelphia 76ers

1981-82 | Los Angeles Lakers

1980-81 | Boston Celtics

1979-80 | Los Angeles Lakers

1978-79 | Seattle SuperSonics

1977-78 | Washington Bullets

1976-77 | Portland Trail Blazers

1975-76 | Boston Celtics

1974-75 | Golden State Warriors

1973-74 | Boston Celtics

1972-73 | New York Knicks

1971-72 | Los Angeles Lakers

1970-71 | Milwaukee Bucks

1969-70 | New York Knicks

1968-69 | Boston Celtics

1967-68 | Boston Celtics

1966-67 | Philadelphia 76ers

1965–66 | Boston Celtics
1964–65 | Boston Celtics
1963–64 | Boston Celtics
1962–63 | Boston Celtics
1961–62 | Boston Celtics
1960–61 | Boston Celtics
1959–60 | Boston Celtics
1958–59 | Boston Celtics
1957–58 | St. Louis Hawks
1956–57 | Boston Celtics
1955–56 | Philadelphia Warriors
1954–55 | Syracuse Nationals
1953–54 | Minneapolis Lakers
1952–53 | Minneapolis Lakers
1951–52 | Minneapolis Lakers
1950–51 | Rochester Royals
1949–50 | Minneapolis Lakers
1948–49 | Minneapolis Lakers
1947–48 | Baltimore Bullets
1946–47 | Philadelphia Warriors

Bill Russell
11 championships

PHOTO CREDITS

ACKNOWLEDGMENTS

This book is dedicated to the greatest physical education teacher of all-time: Coach Jeff Norris. You taught me the value of teamwork, gave me the confidence to excel in not just sports, but in life, and made me a lifelong fan of Australian Rules Football. Go Pies!

Thank you to my wife, Colleen, my entire family, and all my friends for understanding deadlines are a real thing and not just in the movies! Thanks to Ken, Matt, Jeff (and the listeners of *Triviality*); Lauren (and the listeners of *Curated by Chance*); and Erica for your support. To my literary Splash Brother, Justin Brouckaert of Aevitas Creative Management, thanks for the assists. Katie McGuire, my talented editor, your constant alley-oops helped make this book a slam dunk. Nicole James, thanks for drafting me. To everyone at becker&mayer! kids, thanks for letting me kick off this totally awesome new series. To the design team, you made a book I would have bought at my own childhood book fair—the greatest compliment I can give. And last, but not least, thank you to Steph Curry for proving that nice guys don't have to finish last and that hard work does indeed pay off.

ABOUT THE AUTHOR

NEAL E. FISCHER is a former band geek, theater nerd, and prom king, and he was raised on movies totally inappropriate for a five-year-old. (Turned out just fine!) He loves all things pop culture and is known to dominate your favorite trivia night. He was even a contestant on season two of Rob Lowe's game show, *The Floor*. Neal is a former children's theater director and the author of the children's books *The Totally Awesome World of MrBeast* and *The Totally Awesome World of Cristiano Ronaldo*, among many other pop culture titles on a variety of subjects. He wishes he could grow facial hair and once offered Tom Cruise dinner. Neal lives in Chicago with his wife, Colleen, a theater director and special education instructor.

First published in 2025 by becker&mayer!kids, an imprint of The Quarto Group, 142 West 36th Street, 4th Floor, New York, NY 10018, USA
(212) 779-4972 • www.Quarto.com

becker&mayer!kids titles are also available at discount for retail, wholesale, promotional, and bulk purchase. For details, contact the Special Sales Manager by email at specialsales@quarto.com or by mail at The Quarto Group, Attn: Special Sales Manager, 100 Cummings Center Suite 265D, Beverly, MA 01915 USA.

10 9 8 7 6 5 4 3 2 1

ISBN: 978-0-7603-9541-7

Digital edition published in 2025
eISBN: 978-0-7603-9542-4

Library of Congress Control Number: 2024947547

Group Publisher: Rage Kindelsperger
Creative Director: Laura Drew
Managing Editor: Cara Donaldson
Editor: Katie McGuire
Text: Neal E. Fischer
Cover Illustration: Jamie Coe
Cover Design: Scott Richardson
Interior Design: Brad Norr Design

Printed in China

Lexile® 1160L